**Heady ... rry the sleeping child out to his SUV.**

As she did, devouring the view, her gaze riveted to the man she was about to see much more of, she realize[illegible] that somewhere deep down, on a level that was pu[illegible]ly instinctive and primitive and absolutely out of he[illegible] control, she might be experiencing an attraction to [illegible]n.

A[illegible] ttraction she didn't want to have.

A[illegible] ttraction she *couldn't* have, especially not now th[illegible] she was in the same position with him that her m[illegible]er had been with his father once upon a time.

# IT'S A BOY!

BY
VICTORIA PADE

First published in Great Britain 2013
by Mills & Boon, an imprint of Harlequin (UK) Limited,
Eton House, 18-24 Paradise Road, Richmond, Surrey TW9 1SR



ISBN: 978 0 263 90137 5
ebook ISBN: 978 1 472 00521 2

23-0813

Harlequin (UK) policy is to use papers that are natural, renewable and recyclable products and made from wood grown in sustainable forests. The logging and manufacturing processes conform to the legal environmental regulations of the country of origin.

Printed and bound in Spain
by Blackprint CPI, Barcelona

**Victoria Pade** is a *USA TODAY* bestselling author of numerous romance novels. She has two beautiful and talented daughters—Cori and Erin—and is a native of Colorado, where she lives and writes. A devoted chocolate lover, she's in search of the perfect chocolate-chip-cookie recipe.

For information about her latest and upcoming releases, and to find recipes for some of the decadent desserts her characters enjoy, log on to www.vikkipade.com.

To the real Carter.
Such a character and so much fun. You're just great!

## *Chapter One*

"No, Carter, you can't eat cheesecake with your hands!" The man groaned. "Oh, sure, now scratch your head with cheesecake hands. Great. Perfect. Cheesecake in the hair. Can you just stop? Please..."

Heddy Hanrahan was witnessing the fiasco of an intensely hunky business-suit-clad man ineptly dealing with a little boy Heddy guessed to be about two years old.

They were sitting at a table in her small cheesecake shop. And since they were her only customers late on that Monday afternoon, and the man was having such trouble with the very, very cute little boy with the big blue eyes and the now-cheesecake-laced light brown hair, it was difficult for her not to keep glancing in their direction.

To distract herself, she turned her back to them and faced the mirror that lined the wall behind her counter.

This time it was her own reflection that she looked at. And it seemed to her that worry marked her face.

She'd hoped that business would pick up when the magazine article came out saying that her cheesecakes were Colorado's best. And it had. But only slightly. And now that it had been two weeks since the article, she was back to business as usual.

And business as usual meant that business was almost nonexistent.

Which was not good.

She raised her eyebrows to relax the line that sometimes formed between them, then lowered them to their usual position over her hazel-colored eyes.

Her situation was bad enough—she didn't need wrinkles, too.

She also thought that worry was making her ordinarily fair skin even paler than it normally was, which wasn't good, either. The fair skin came with her dark copper-colored hair and it didn't take much to wash her out. The last thing she wanted was to be the same color as her cheesecakes, so she pinched her cheeks and made a mental note to use more blush tomorrow.

Her hair *was* her best asset, though, so she accepted the fair skin as a trade-off. The dark russet locks that fell to five inches below her shoulders were thick and curly—not kinky-curly but wavy-curly. Enough so that even when her hair was pulled up—the way she always wore it in the shop or when she was making the cheesecakes—it was full and just slightly billowy, gently framing her face without being stark.

Although it was a mystery to her why not looking stark mattered so much to her at this moment…

Certainly it couldn't have anything to do with the attractive man who was her customer because that would just be ridiculous.

She turned away from the mirror and made herself appear busy, leaning into her display case and needlessly adjusting the assortment of cheesecakes that she sold whole or by the slice.

Too many of them were still uncut, but she tried not to let worry creep in again. She had customers, she told herself, that was something....

Glancing through the glass front of the display case, she saw the man using paper napkins in a feeble attempt to get the cheesecake out of the child's hair. Because he was too intent on that to realize she was watching, she went on watching as she stood again, making sure as she did that the white blouse she had tucked into her jeans was still tucked in in back.

There just wasn't anything else for her *to* do but monitor her lone customers. It wasn't as if she couldn't keep her eyes off the man. Despite the fact that he was one of the best-looking men she'd ever seen. Things like that didn't matter to her.

But he *was* one of the best-looking men she'd ever seen.

He had dark, dark brown hair the color of espresso-laced chocolate, cut short on the sides and only a bit longer on top where it was left slightly messy.

His eyes were as rich a blue as blueberries—even more intense and striking a blue than the little boy's eyes. His brow was very square, and his nose was perfectly straight and just the right length.

He had lips that somehow managed to strike Heddy as sexy and a jawline chiseled enough to cut bread.

Plus, when he'd first walked in she'd been struck by how tall he was—at least an inch or two over six feet. He had wonderfully broad shoulders and what appeared to be a muscular physique under a suit that was so well-tailored she couldn't imagine why he'd worn it if he knew he was going to wrangle a child.

"Terrific. Two fists full of cheesecake in the mouth at once," the intensely handsome man muttered.

Heddy saw the little boy doing just that: eating cheesecake out of both hands by turns, his head swiveling back and forth between them as if he were eating an ear of corn. She couldn't help smiling at the child's clear appreciation of her cheesecake.

He was an adorable kid, she noted as well, just to prove to herself that she wasn't focusing unduly on the man. The little boy was dressed like a miniature lumberjack in imitation work boots, tiny jeans with cuffs at the ankles and a plaid flannel shirt. Somewhere along the way the man had thought to push the sleeves of the shirt up to the child's elbows and the toddler was also wearing a plastic wristwatch on each wrist—one watch bright yellow, the other baby blue.

The silliness of those two wristwatches made her smile. A sad-feeling smile. But anything to do with kids made her sad; that was why she tried not to pay too much attention to them. It was just too painful for her.

At least this particular child was a boy not a girl….

He resembled the man somewhat—certainly not in the cheeks that were chubby rather than chiseled—but around the eyes and nose. Enough to tell her they were probably related. But because there was nothing about the way the man acted with the child to suggest they were close, she assumed he wasn't the little boy's father. Maybe he was an uncle, pinch-hitting at caregiving for the child's mother or father.

But whoever these two were, it was gratifying to see how much the little boy seemed to like her white chocolate mousse cheesecake when he picked up the empty plate to lick it and then said gleefully, "More!"

The man glanced in Heddy's direction and smiled an embarrassed smile that was no less knee-weakening because of the embarrassment. Not that her knees were weakened or that it mattered either…

"I guess I was wrong and one piece was not enough for us to share. I'm sorry for the mess we're making, but can we have another round? Maybe we'll try a slice of the raspberry white chocolate mousse this time."

"Sure," Heddy responded.

Glad for an additional sale and for something to do, she took out one of the knives she kept in hot water. Drying the heated blade, she used it to cut the cheesecake he'd requested.

Then she dampened a clean cloth in warm water from the tap behind her counter and brought it with the cheesecake to the customer's table. She set the plate out of the toddler's reach—something it hadn't occurred to the man to do—before she offered the man the wet towel and said, "You can use this like a washcloth. It'll probably work better than dry napkins to clean him up."

"I think I just need a hose," her customer muttered, accepting the wet cloth anyway and thanking her for it.

Then he said, "You wouldn't happen to be Heddy Hanrahan, would you?"

"That's me," she said, struck suddenly that there might be something vaguely familiar about him. But only vaguely. Maybe he'd been in the shop before.

Then he said, "I'm Lang Camden."

"As in Camden Superstores?"

"That's us."

A Camden.

Oh, dear…

That was why he seemed vaguely familiar. The Camden family not only owned Camden Superstores but any number of buildings, businesses, factories, warehouses, production facilities, trucks and who-knew-what-else in conjunction with those stores. The chain was worldwide and the family's name appeared annually at or near the top of lists of the richest people in the United States.

Their wealth and renown caused pictures of one Camden or another to show up in the newspaper or magazines from time to time. There were so many of them—ten descendants of the man who had built the empire, plus their grandmother—that it wasn't as if Heddy knew them by sight. But because the Camden name was a name her mother and grandfather were once disastrously connected with, a name she'd heard cursed innumerable times during her life, curiosity always caused Heddy to take more interest in those pictures and the articles that went with them than she might have otherwise. So she assumed she'd probably seen this man's face a time or two in print somewhere.

"Can we talk?" he asked.

Curiosity about why a Camden would want to talk to her caused her to say a tentative, "Okay."

"Will you sit with us? Maybe over there, out of the line of fire." He nodded at the chair across the table from him and from the toddler, who was now standing on his own chair to lean over and reach for the second slice of cheesecake.

As Heddy went to the opposite side of the café table she pointed to the cheesecake and said, "You're about to lose that."

Quick reflexes on Lang Camden's part slid the dessert plate out of the little boy's reach just in time. Then he caught him around the middle and seated him again.

"More!" the toddler demanded.

The child's inept caregiver picked up one of the clean spoons Heddy had brought with the sccond slice and used it to taste thc raspberry white chocolate mousse cheesecake. Then he fed a bite to the child with the other clean spoon.

"Mmm..." was the child's assessment before he opened his mouth for his second bite.

"This is Carter," Lang Camden said in a flustered voice, still giving her no clue as to who Carter was to him. "He's two and a half and, as you can probably tell, a big fan of your cheesecake. With good reason—what I've tasted so far is fantastic."

"Thank you," Heddy said, wondering more by the minute what had brought a member of the illustrious Camden family to her shop in suburban Arcada. And hoping that her mother wouldn't choose this moment for one of her numerous drop-in visits. Heddy had no doubt that her mother coming face-to-face with a Camden would not be a good thing.

"We saw the article on your shop," Lang Camden said then, as if he knew what she was thinking.

"'The Best Cheesecake in Denver That No One Is Eating'?" Heddy asked, reciting the title of the piece that had gone on to say that even after extensive testing by a panel of the magazine's staff, her cheesecakes had been judged the best that the entire state had to offer.

"That's the one," Lang Camden confirmed as he took another bite of the dessert and Carter protested with a "Mine!"

"Okay, okay," Lang Camden conceded, giving in and sliding the plate to the two-and-a-half-year-old, letting him dive in the way he wanted to.

"How many different variations of cheesecake do you make?" the older of Heddy's two customers asked then, turning the full focus of those striking blue eyes on her.

"Oh, a lot. I do the mousse cheesecakes and also traditional baked cheesecakes. And besides the most common things like plain, blueberry and raspberry, I try to do what's in season. Since it's the start of April we're getting into spring fruits. I change things up from week to week, and there are a few savory cheesecakes I make, too, but those are special orders."

He nodded. "We're about to launch a division of gourmet foods in Camden Superstores," he informed her. "What would you say to providing your cheesecakes as part of that?"

Taken completely off guard, for a moment Heddy was speechless. Then the only thing she could think to say was, "You're kidding."

"Nope, not kidding."

Heddy heard herself make a sound that was part laugh, part huff. The idea was absurd in so many ways.

"This shop used to be only my house," she said. "The city allows these old homes on Main Street to be lived in or to act as places of business. In my case, it's both. I turned my basement into a kitchen space just big enough to make the cheesecakes I sell. Where we're sitting used to be my living room and sunporch, now it's my shop. I live in what's left—the back half and the upstairs. There's no way—*no* way—I could ever make enough cheesecakes to supply even one Camden Superstore."

Not to mention that she already knew much, much too well that the type of arrangement he was suggesting had a history of actually destroying a small business like hers.

"Actually, we'd want to start with all of the Colorado stores at first, then eventually we'd want to expand to put your cheesecakes in every store around the world. And we'd want them to be exclusive to Camden Superstores."

He really couldn't be serious with this.

But he'd said it with a straight face.

Maybe he just wasn't aware of the catastrophe that had befallen her family's bakery because of doing business like this with his family in the past. It *had* been years and years ago, long before Heddy was born, before her mother had even met her father. Probably long before Lang Camden had been born, too, since he looked to be her age—thirty or not much past it. She supposed that it was possible that he had no idea that her mother and her grandfather had made a deal with the devil—

as her mother liked to put it—and paid for it with their livelihood as well as her mother's broken heart.

Regardless of the harsh lessons of the past and whether or not Lang Camden knew about what had happened, it seemed more than clear to Heddy that she couldn't accommodate what he was proposing, so that was the tack she stuck to.

"Again, I couldn't begin to meet your needs."

Why had something about that sounded a tad suggestive? She hadn't intended for it to. And apparently she wasn't the only one to have heard it because it brought a smile to Lang Camden's handsome face.

But he made no comment and instead went on to say, "I know that at least part of what makes you leery is that a deal similar to this cost your family their bread business."

So he *did* know....

"That's why we want to do things differently this time around," he continued. "We'll provide the financing in the form of a grant for you to expand production—"

"'A grant'?" Heddy interjected.

"A grant," he repeated. "Not a loan, not even a partial subsidy. It won't cost you a penny and it will still be your business. The facility will be in your name alone. You'll own it outright, and the whole thing will still be your baby."

Skepticism and suspicion set in.

"That seems a little too good to be true," Heddy told him point-blank.

"I don't know why, there are grants for a lot of things—education, small businesses, housing..."

"Maybe from the government, but—"

"There are private grants, too. Camden Inc. gives several of them."

"Like this? On this scale?" Heddy asked with a full measure of disbelief in her voice.

"I will always be perfectly straight with you," he said as if he were making a vow. "Yes, this *is* the first time we've done a grant on this scale. But that doesn't change the terms. A grant goes out free and clear to the recipient—in this case, to you. And I come with it."

He added that with a smile that was so engaging it was hard for Heddy to maintain her grip on reality. "You come with it?" she said, hating whatever it was in her tone that almost sounded as though that made the offer more tempting. Which of course it didn't.

"You'll have my personal guidance as Camden Inc.'s start-up guy to establish and staff a commercial kitchen big enough to produce the supply we need. I'll make sure that you grow to whatever extent is required to meet demand, and that you're up and running effectively and efficiently before I leave you on your own so that history doesn't repeat itself."

Again, too good to be true.

"Where's the catch?" Heddy asked.

"I guess if there's any *catch* at all, it's in the exclusivity. Camden Superstores will be the only place to get your cheesecakes. But other than that—"

"If they don't sell, you won't carry them and I'll be through."

"No-oo," he assured her. "You'll have a contract with us. If they don't sell, we'll nullify the contract and you'll be free to sell somewhere else—grocery stores, restaurants, whatever. You'll still have the capacity for mass production that you don't have here, so you'll still have the chance to keep going. But I can't imagine why your cheesecakes wouldn't sell through us. Especially since you'll have our marketing and advertising division behind you, and cheesecakes in a worldwide chain of stores that are never hurting for sales."

It still seemed too good to be true to Heddy but she couldn't find the actual flaw so she merely shook her head in continuing disbelief.

"It will all be drawn up legally," Lang Camden said then. "And you can have whatever lawyers or advisors you want to review the terms for anything that might cause you concern. But let's face it…" He glanced around and, with a sympathetically wrinkled brow, said, "You gave a party here and no one came. What I'm offering you is a way to still do this but on a larger scale and at no cost to you except to throw in the towel on this place. And let it go back to just being your house."

Still trying to figure out what the downside was in this, Heddy saw Carter stand on his chair again and lean onto the table to lick the second empty cheesecake plate. Only this time he was tipping the chair and instinct made Heddy jump to her feet and lunge to catch him.

Lang Camden's reflex was to reach for the chair and steady it, and together they kept the child from falling.

"Carter…" Lang Camden groaned again.

"Good pie," the toddler responded. "More!"

"I think you've had your limit. But we'll buy one to take home," the obviously inept caregiver promised.

"The ra'berry one," Carter demanded enthusiastically.

The older of her two customers again sat the child

in the chair. Then he used the wet towel in another attempt to clean him up.

"Wash lallow Zsorzse," Carter instructed, holding out one arm where cheesecake smudged the face of his yellow wristwatch.

"'Zsorzse'?" Heddy repeated.

"George. He's obsessed with Curious George, but he pronounces g's like…I don't know, like the way you say Zsa Zsa Gabor."

"And he tells so much time he needs *two* watches?" Heddy asked.

"He's obsessed with watches, too. Don't ask me why. And some kind of weird toy with a stuffed animal head and a body that's just a small blanket. He calls that Baby and he *has* to have it somewhere near at all times. We left Baby in the car but at any minute the fact that it isn't in here could become a crisis."

"Baby's nappin'," Carter said as if the man was deluded. Then to Heddy, the child said, "More pie?"

"It's cheesecake, Carter," Lang Camden amended.

"Not *cheese*. Pie!" the two-and-a-half-year-old shouted.

Lang Camden sighed and gave up washing the cherubic face before getting it completely clean because Carter had wiggled out of his ineffective grasp.

Now that he was free, the little boy slid off the chair, went to Heddy's display case and licked it the way he'd licked the cheesecake plates.

"Carter," Lang Camden moaned in complaint. "Don't do that!"

"Big food," Carter said by way of explanation.

Lang Camden rolled his eyes. "I don't know what

goes through his head. He doesn't usually go around licking everything. I guess he thinks the whole place tastes good."

"It's okay," Heddy said. "I'm flattered that he likes the cheesecakes so much that he even wants to eat the display case."

"Maybe we'll use him as an endorsement—that is, if you're interested in my proposition...."

Again, there was a slightly suggestive inflection but Heddy was reasonably sure he hadn't intended it because he caught himself and added, "My business proposition."

Once more Heddy shook her head. "I just don't—"

"Tell me you aren't going under here, Heddy," he challenged. "I can see for myself that you are, and that's basically what that article said. The cheesecakes are great but not enough people are buying them."

"Still..."

"No, not 'still.' I came here today to make sure the product is worth selling. It is, and my family wants to help you sell it. I'm not talking about buying you out. It'll continue to be your business and the worst thing that can happen is that you'll bomb out at Camden Superstores but end up with the ability to sell on a large scale to any number of other places. Or you can sell the facility and equipment to bankroll something else. If you want, I'll even have something written up that promises my guidance to get you started over in that something else. It's a no-lose deal I'm offering you."

"And why is that?" Heddy asked outright.

He sighed as if he had to say something he was hoping he wouldn't have to say. "We know that years ago your family signed on to provide bread for the Camden stores that were around then. We know that your supply couldn't keep up with our demand. We know that by the time everyone realized that, and my father and the rest of the family in charge back then decided to make other arrangements, your family had lost all of their other customers so they were left with no business at all."

Not to mention the personal side of the situation that had taken its toll on her mother. Did he know about *that,* too?

Heddy reined in her wandering thoughts as he said, "We wouldn't want to do business with you if your product wasn't worth selling. But it is, so we *do* want to do business with you. We just want to make sure that the mistakes of the past aren't repeated."

"It just seems—"

"I know, you said it. Too good to be true. But that's kind of how grants are, aren't they? Money for free. You have a product we want. The grant will let you produce enough of that product to meet our needs and provide you with a better situation—you make more cheesecakes, we sell more of your cheesecakes, we both win. And one way or another, you don't lose, which you're on the verge of doing now."

"Wan that *big* one!" Carter announced from the front of the display case.

Heddy used the interruption as an excuse to get up and go behind the counter while she continued to try to figure out what dangers and disadvantages there might be in this.

Lang got up and followed her, remaining on the customer's side of the display case with Carter and agreeing to buy the largest cheesecake.

While Heddy boxed it for them, Lang said, "Sleep on it. If you have a business consultant, talk to your business consultant about it. If anything still bothers you, we can talk it over, do whatever it takes to make you feel comfortable doing business with us again. But we really want this to work."

Because her cheesecakes were that good or because the Camdens had another motive that would benefit them and potentially harm her?

Heddy believed her cheesecakes were that good.

But she also knew better than most people how treacherous the Camdens had been in the past, and how easy it was to be caught under the wheels of Camden progress and turned into nothing but road kill.

"Just think it over," Lang urged as he handed her his credit card.

Heddy made no promises as she ran the card and had him sign the slip.

"I'll be in touch," he said as he accepted the card and the receipt. "But you have my word and whatever guarantees you want that I can make this work for you. That I *will* make this work for you if you'll let me."

"I'll think about it," Heddy finally conceded. But that was all she was conceding because she was also beginning to think about what her mother's reaction to this would be. It wouldn't be good….

"Get your coat, Carter," Lang told the toddler, and Heddy was surprised to see the child comply.

"Pie in car?" Carter asked as he let the older man put on his coat.

"No pie in the car. Tonight, if you eat your dinner, maybe you can have another piece then."

"Pie in car," Carter said as if that were far more reasonable.

"Looks like the cheesecake rides home in the trunk," Lang confided in Heddy.

"Better the cheesecake than the child," Heddy said with some humor.

"Are you sure?" Lang joked in return.

"Reasonably..."

He laughed and palmed the top of Carter's head like a basketball with his left hand, which Heddy just happened to notice sported no wedding ring.

Not that that mattered to her either.

"Come on, Carter man, let's get you home," Lang said, guiding the child to the door. Just before he went out, the tall man glanced at Heddy over his shoulder and repeated, "I'll be in touch."

Heddy merely nodded, watching him clumsily put the cheesecake in the rear compartment of a large SUV and then get Carter settled in his car seat in the row ahead of that.

As she looked on, she thought about what Lang Camden had just offered her and wondered if this was an answer to her prayers, or if the devil in a business suit had just placed the same temptation in front of her that had sunk her family once before.

One thing was certain, though, she thought as she watched him get behind the wheel. Lang Camden was a handsome devil. A handsome, handsome devil.

And she was just glad that, unlike her mother, that couldn't get to her. It couldn't have any kind of real effect on her at all.

Because she was still Daniel's wife and she would always be Daniel's wife.

Even if there wasn't a Daniel anymore....

## *Chapter Two*

"Come on, Carter, let's let GiGi and your dad talk. We can roll balls into the pockets on the pool table."

"Poo-al," Carter repeated before he jumped down from the seat of the enormous breakfast nook in Georgianna Camden's kitchen. He left with Jonah Morrison, the elderly man who'd recently become the constant companion to the matriarch of the Camden family.

That left Lang alone with his grandmother.

"*Dad!* I don't think I'll ever get used to anyone calling me that," Lang muttered.

GiGi laughed. "Oh, believe me, you will. There'll come a day when someone in a crowd will yell 'Dad' and you'll answer before you remember that you don't even have Carter with you."

"I think it's more likely that I'll be in a crowd and forget that I actually do have him with me," Lang countered.

"He needs a bath and his hair washed," GiGi decreed.

"Yeah, tonight."

"That's pie in his hair?"

"Cheesecake. From Heddy Hanrahan's shop—we were there yesterday. Carter calls it pie. He got into the refrigerator when I was already late for work this morning, and went straight for the cheesecake with his bare hands. Some of it ended up in his hair. There was nothing I could do about it then. Heddy Hanrahan's cheesecake gets a stamp of approval from us both, by the way—that's what I came over to talk to you about. I made her the offer."

GiGi ignored what Lang said and continued on the subject of Carter's hygiene.

"That boy has been walking around all day long with cheesecake in his hair?" the older woman said disapprovingly.

"Hey, you and Jani and Lindie and Livi left me in the lurch, remember? No more help from you, no more help from cousin Jani, no more help from my two sisters. That means my hands are full."

"So he went around all day today with cheesecake in his hair," GiGi concluded.

"I could have brought him here. You could have given him a bath and washed his hair while I was at work, and then my day would have been a lot better and he'd be clean," Lang pointed out, his frustration ringing in his voice. "But—"

"No," GiGi said with a stubborn shake of her head.

"Couldn't you and the girls take care of him the way you have been just until I can hire a nanny? Or two? He's such a handful, he'll probably need more than one."

GiGi shook her head again and said another firm no. "Your sisters, your cousin and I have been the *only* ones taking care of him since he came to you three months ago, Lang. That was in *January* and now this is *April.* He's your son. We're all proud of you for stepping up and doing the right thing, but now you have to actually *do* it. You need time with that boy. You need to become more than just a biological father."

"I know, I know," Lang conceded, feeling guilty for how much he'd relied on his grandmother, his sisters and his cousin since taking Carter on. "But twenty-four hours a day, seven days a week? I need some help and my secretary isn't moving any too quickly in finding it for me."

Lang had his suspicions that his family had gotten to his secretary and told her to drag her feet so that he was forced to care for Carter for a while. And *because* he now had constant child care and a job to do—and the deal with Heddy Hanrahan on top of it all—there was just no way he could beat the bushes for a nanny himself.

"You know that the Camden name can attract trouble," his grandmother pointed out, running her hand through her salt-and-pepper hair. "Whoever gets hired as your nanny has to be above reproach for Carter's safety and security. Even after your secretary finds likely candidates, they have to be put through a thorough background check and that takes time."

"Yeah, I know," Lang said with a sigh.

He was annoyed with the delay but he knew what his grandmother was saying was true. He couldn't risk handing Carter over to just any child-care provider and getting back a ransom note. In their position there was always cause for caution. Money made them targets in many ways.

"But if you and Jonah and Margaret and Louie could just watch him on weekdays—" Lang persisted.

"No, Lang." GiGi held the line.

Margaret and Louie were the house staff who had long ago become more like members of the family than employees. They were GiGi's closest friends and had helped her raise all ten of her grandchildren after the plane crash that had killed their parents. They'd also provided more than their fair share of Carter's care for the past three months.

"Carter is *your* child," his grandmother went on. "But since taking him you've had less to do with him than anyone. It's been just like everything else since Audrey left—you keep anyone new at arm's length. But that boy *is* family. *Your* family, and you can't stay closed off from him—it'll be a disaster for you both."

"If I had shut myself off and kept everybody since Audrey at arm's length there wouldn't *be* a Carter," Lang pointed out.

"Bull! Carter's mother appealed to you because she wasn't much more than a one-night stand who didn't ask anything of you beyond the physical. It was a fly-by-night imitation of a relationship on the rebound. And since then you haven't even bothered to pretend—all you've had is flings. One-night stands."

"Wow, I am not going to talk about one-night stands with my grandmother," Lang said.

"The point is, you've built a wall around yourself. I know it's protective and gives you the sense that you have the control that you lost with Audrey so you can't get hurt again, but you can't live a full life that way, honey."

"Maybe I'm just holding out for something more."

"If you're holding out for anything, it's Audrey's clone. You've nixed every genuinely nice, substantial girl who's crossed your path for the past three and a half years because something about them didn't measure up to Audrey. And that has to stop!"

He really hadn't come over here tonight to have the riot act read to him.

"Maybe what I'm holding out for is what I *felt* for Audrey and that just hasn't happened." Under his breath he added, "Except the next time I'd like it if the other person feels that way about me, too."

"You aren't going to find that in the kind of women you've been seeing. And in the meantime, you need to open up enough to be a father to that baby."

"Well, the result is that he has cheesecake in his hair," Lang concluded matter-of-factly, and then steered the conversation to what he'd come to his grandmother's house to discuss in the first place. "Because apparently you didn't think it was enough to throw me into the deep end with him, you also thought this would be a good time for me to take my turn at your project of making amends."

Camden Incorporated had been founded and built by Lang's great-grandfather, H. J. Camden. A scrappy man who had been willing to do just about anything to accomplish his goals.

The family loved H.J., and had hoped that the rumors and suspicions that he had been ruthless and unscrupulous were false. They'd also hoped that the suspicions that his son Hank and his two grandsons had acted as H.J.'s henchmen were false, too. But the recent discovery of H.J.'s journals had left them with no illusions. Camden Incorporated had been built by methods the current Camdens weren't proud of.

GiGi and her ten grandchildren had set out to make amends to people harmed by H.J., Hank, Mitchum and Howard's actions, or to the families and descendants who might have suffered as a result.

GiGi decided which of her grandchildren to send on each particular mission. Part of her reasoning being to learn what harm had been done then to offer an opportunity of some kind that might benefit and compensate without appearing to be an outward admission of guilt and an offer of restitution. Their fear was that any public admission of guilt might inspire unwarranted lawsuits against them.

This was why Lang had approached Heddy Hanrahan on Monday.

"Maybe juggling so much will actually be good for you," GiGi said. "Sometimes having your hands full forces the walls to come down."

Lang wondered if his grandmother was thinking about herself when she said that. She had opened up her home and herself to ten grandchildren when they landed on her doorstep. As a result, he, his sisters and cousins had been well cared for and had experienced a warm, loving upbringing. But even if that was what she was trying to accomplish for Carter, Lang was still completely overwhelmed and he couldn't say he liked the position she was putting him in all the way around.

"Now tell me what happened with the Hanrahan girl

so you can get that boy home and cleaned up," GiGi commanded.

Lang saw that nothing he said was going to gain him any help with Carter so he proceeded to outline how his meeting with Heddy Hanrahan had gone for his grandmother.

"I don't think there's any doubt that she's going under if she doesn't take the deal, but she's leery of us," he concluded.

"Of course she would be, it goes with the territory," GiGi said. "But you told her she can have everything in writing?"

"I did. And even though she seemed on the verge of saying no, I got her to think the proposition over. I'm going back after work tomorrow to see what she has to say."

"Do you think she knows about her mother and your father?"

Lang shrugged. "I have no clue. We only talked business. And Carter ate a lot of cheesecake. We tried two varieties, and that magazine article was right—they're terrific. We won't have any problem selling them for sure."

"And beyond the fact that she didn't jump at the chance to go into business with us, how was your reception otherwise?"

"Okay," Lang said. "It wasn't what Jani met from Gideon that first time she approached him. Heddy Hanrahan doesn't seem to hate us the way Gideon did initially."

His cousin Jani had been dispatched on the last of these ventures, and the man she'd encountered during the course of that—Gideon Thatcher—had not been happy to have any contact with a Camden.

"I could tell that Heddy was shocked when I introduced myself," Lang went on, "but she didn't tell us to get out or anything. And when I asked her to sit and talk, she did. She was actually fairly friendly—cautious but nice enough."

"Did you learn anything about her or her family? Is her mother still around? Is she married? Divorced? Widowed?"

"She wasn't wearing a wedding ring."

"You met her mother?"

Somehow they were on different tracks. "No," Lang said, "I didn't meet anyone but Heddy. I meant Heddy wasn't wearing a wedding ring. Her mother wasn't around and didn't come up."

Lang wasn't sure if he'd misunderstood his grandmother because of the way she'd asked the questions or if it was just that he had Heddy Hanrahan on the brain. Because despite the fact that his hands had been full with Carter, his head had been full of Heddy Hanrahan since meeting her.

Thoughts of her had been creeping up on him every time he turned around. Thoughts *and* images of her. Of that lush red hair—not carrot-colored at all, but a deep, dark, rich mahogany red. Beautiful. She had beautiful hair. Wavy and thick.

And it wasn't only her hair that had had him sneaking peeks of her when he should have been keeping closer tabs on Carter—which was how Carter had ended up with cheesecake in his hair in the first place. Heddy Hanrahan also had the most flawless peaches-and-cream skin he'd ever seen, and luminous hazel eyes with bright green flecks.

Plus she had a face that was as delicate as fine china: a gently curved brow; high, pronounced cheekbones; a thin, straight nose; and a mouth that sported such pink kissable lips....

Not that he'd had any thought of kissing her, for crying out loud, because he hadn't. He was just trying to do business with her, to compensate her and maybe the rest of her family, for what had happened to them years ago.

Okay, so he'd also taken enough of a look at her compact little body to know it was great, too—with curves in all the right places—but that didn't mean he'd itched to touch her.

Although yeah, maybe a little part of him had. But it didn't mean anything.

"Heddy Hanrahan didn't mention her mother at all?" GiGi's voice pulled him out of the reverie he'd slipped into.

"No," Lang answered in a hurry, hoping he didn't seem dazed. "We only talked business. You said you couldn't find an obituary for her mother, so she must be around somewhere, but she didn't come up." Then something occurred to him that rocked him. "Heddy Hanrahan couldn't be my half sister, could she?"

"Don't be silly," GiGi chastised. "The article said she was thirty. It's been thirty-six years since Mitchum was involved with her mother. I was just hoping to hear that her mother was still happily married to her father and had had a good life after what went on with your dad."

*A good life after what went on...*

That was what they hoped for in all of these cases—

to discover that the people burned by dealing with the Camdens in the past had gone on to bigger and better things and not suffered long-term negative effects.

"So she's pretty, is she?" GiGi said then.

"Beautiful," Lang said, putting it out front so GiGi couldn't think it made any difference to him. "Why? Would we not be offering her this deal if she was homely as hell?"

GiGi smiled a smile that irked him because it seemed to say that she saw through him. But she was wrong. He wasn't interested in Heddy Hanrahan the woman. He might not agree with his family's assessment that he'd closed himself off, but he certainly had enough on his hands right now without adding romance or a relationship or even another one-night stand.

Although he really, really would like to see that rust-colored hair down....

But he was always sort of a sucker for a redhead, so that didn't mean anything, either.

He didn't want to talk any more about Heddy Hanrahan or her looks with his grandmother, though, so he raised his chin in the direction that Jonah had taken Carter and shouted, "Carter! Come on, we need to get home!" Then, wanting to give his grandmother a little of what she'd dished out, he said to GiGi, "We'd better get going so you can have your evening alone with your old high school squeeze. Seems like he might as well move in, he's here so much."

"It's in discussion," GiGi said.

"Really..." Lang countered with raised eyebrows. "Is that why you won't babysit for me? You're too busy getting busy with—"

"*I* am not going to talk about *that* with my grandson!" GiGi said with a laugh, echoing what he'd said to her earlier about one-night stands.

"Ooo-hoo, GiGi's gettin' busy…" Lang teased. And he actually thought his grandmother's ordinarily pink cheeks might have turned a shade pinker.

Sliding out of the breakfast nook, he went around to the other side where GiGi was sitting and leaned close to her ear. "It better be more *substantial* than a one-night stand," he goaded playfully before he kissed her on the cheek.

She swatted his arm and said just as playfully, "Mind your manners!"

No chance. Lang decided to be incorrigible. "Shall I have a talk with him? Make sure his intentions are honorable?"

"What makes you think mine are?"

Lang laughed and straightened. He did love the old bird even if she had taken him to task tonight.

"Come on, Carter," he shouted again just before Jonah Morrison herded the toddler back into the kitchen. "Let's go. We have to pick up some dinner so we can eat fast and get you a bath and wash your hair. I'm thinking pizza tonight."

"Wis 'napple!" Carter contributed.

"Only on your part. I don't like pineapple on my pizza."

"Look how good you're getting—you knew what he was saying," GiGi praised.

Lang merely rolled his eyes and shook his head before he put on Carter's coat and they all went to the front door.

"Let me know what happens tomorrow with the beautiful Heddy Hanrahan," GiGi called after him as he led Carter out, clearly getting Lang back with a jab of her own.

"I will," he answered just before he hoisted Carter into his car seat.

But the mere mention of Heddy was all it took for the picture of her to pop back into his head—and there was no denying that she *was* beautiful.

It just didn't have anything to do with anything.

And neither did the small feeling of eagerness that ran through him at the thought of seeing her again tomorrow.

Because while he would never admit it to his grandmother or any of the rest of his family, even if he didn't have learning to be a father to Carter on his plate right now, he wasn't ready to let another woman in.

Not even one with red hair.

And he wasn't sure he ever would be....

"I've gone over your books backward and forward, Heddy, and I wish I could tell you something else. But the honest, ugly truth is that you've been open for fifteen months and this shop is not making it."

Heddy had called her cousin Clair on Monday night after closing up to tell her about the visit from Lang Camden. Clair was a certified public accountant and she did Heddy's books as a favor to Heddy. Now, late on Wednesday afternoon, Clair had showed up with those books to present to Heddy on paper how her business was going under.

"You used the lion's share of Daniel's life insurance

money to start the business," Clair continued. "You've had to draw on the rest for working and living expenses because you haven't made a profit a single month since you opened last year, so what's left is just about gone. Is there any reason to think you'll have a turnaround and business will pick up?"

"I hoped that the article would do it but it hasn't. So no," Heddy admitted.

"Then I say take the deal from the Camdens," Clair concluded. "Protect yourself but take it. Clark can draw up papers or look over anything the Camdens come up with to make sure everything's to your advantage. You know how competitive my husband is, and he's dying to go head-to-head with the big-boy Camden team of attorneys. But, sweetie, it's either that or go back to nursing."

Heddy shook her head. "I can't do that," she said with the same edge of near-panic that the idea had given her since she'd left pediatric nursing after that awful night that had cost her so dearly. "I can't even stand the *thought* of going back to working with kids—of being close to *any* kids, sick or well. No way."

"You know the fact that you were a nurse and on duty that night isn't to blame. And whether or not it's the way you want it, working that night actually *saved* you," Clair said compassionately.

It was the same thing her cousin had said numerous times in the past five years.

"You could go into some other area of nursing—you were so good…"

More fierce head-shaking. "No. Maybe it doesn't seem logical or reasonable—or even sane—to you, but

I can't go back to doing what I was doing that night. These stupid cheesecakes were my salvation."

Clair sighed. "Then take the Camden's offer," she reiterated as if there was no other advice she could give. "Clark and I will keep an eye on your side to make sure what happened to your mom and your grandfather doesn't happen to you. If it's set up the way it was laid out to you, even if the Camdens do bail, what Lang Camden said is right—you can sell to grocery stores or restaurants. That still puts you in a better position than you're in now."

That was how Heddy saw it, too. Despite trying to talk herself out of it since Monday when she'd watched the hauntingly handsome Lang Camden leave.

"But there's still Mom," Heddy said direly. "I haven't told her anything about this yet. You know she'll hit the ceiling."

"You can't blame her. But still—"

Heddy and Clair were sitting at one of the tables in the shop—Heddy with her back to the door, Clair facing it—when the shop door opened.

"My second customer of this whole day," Heddy muttered to her cousin, wondering why Clair's jaw dropped when she glanced at whoever had just come in.

When Heddy got up to tend to the customer, she saw it was Lang Camden, with Carter in tow again.

"Oh," Heddy said, understanding her cousin's expression.

"Hi." Lang greeted the two women with a smile.

He was dressed in another business suit. This time it was a dark grayish-blue, with a pale blue shirt and matching tie. While Heddy had been tormented by the recurring mental image of the man far, far more than she'd wanted to be since Monday, she was somehow struck all over again by how drop-dead gorgeous he was.

"Hi," Heddy said after a pause. "Uh…Clair, this is Lang Camden. Mr. Camden, this is my cousin and best friend—and accountant—Clair Darnell."

"Call me Lang," he amended. "Nice to meet you, Clair. I hope you're here in all your capacities to persuade Heddy to do business with me."

Clair was jolted back into the moment. "We've talked," she said without giving anything away. Then she gathered her purse and a file folder from the table and said to Heddy, "I have to get going, but let me know what you decide. And if you want, I can be there when you tell your mom…."

"Thanks," Heddy responded as Lang followed his eager little boy companion to the display case and Heddy walked with Clair to the door.

Once they were there, Clair leaned close to Heddy's ear and whispered, "You didn't tell me he *looked* like that! I could leave home for him."

Heddy laughed softly, as if his good looks didn't affect her—which was a long way from the truth. Not only was she unable to stop thinking about him, she'd even dreamed about him. Three times in only two nights…

"You wouldn't leave Clark for anyone," she whispered back to her cousin.

"Don't be too sure," Clair muttered as she peered over Heddy's shoulder for a second glimpse. "And the kid?"

"I don't know who he is. He was with him before, too," Heddy said just as Carter announced loudly that he wanted "burberry" pie.

"You better get over there. Call me," Clair said, sneaking another look at the man as she left.

"I wan burberry pie," Carter repeated to Heddy as she went behind the counter to face Lang and the boy.

"I think that means blueberry," Lang said uncertainly. "Let's hope so, anyway. Give us a slice of the blueberry white chocolate mousse. And today I'll have a slice of the plain New Jersey. Is that the basic, traditional, baked variety?"

"It is," Heddy confirmed, taking out both as-yet-uncut cheesecakes to slice.

"Then will you come and sit with us?"

"Sure," Heddy agreed, feeling a rush of butterflies to her stomach.

She wasn't sure if the tension was coming from the fact that she was seriously considering taking the leap and accepting his business proposal, a leap that would not be well received by her family. Or if it was just having Lang Camden in her shop again—tall and lean with that dark, dark hair artfully tousled and that hint of scruffy whiskers on that sharp jawline.

He was as sexy in the flesh as he'd been in those unwelcome dreams she'd had of him.

He got Carter situated at the table nearest to the display case and Heddy brought over the two slices of cheesecake. Then she sat across from them and watched as the little boy, who had on jeans and a crew-necked sweater, grabbed the spoon and scooped up a bite too big for his mouth, opening wide in a feeble attempt to get it all in.

"Gooo," he mumbled around what he had managed to accommodate.

Lang Camden used his own spoon for a bite of Carter's cheesecake, confirmed the child's opinion, then tried his own slice.

He let his eyes roll back into his handsome head and moaned. "And I thought the mousse ones were good! That's the richest, creamiest... It's terrific."

Heddy smiled. "I'm glad."

"So tell me you're going to let me sell these," he said then, without any more preamble.

Heddy didn't answer him immediately.

She wasn't sure about her grandfather but she knew that her mother would have a fit if she said yes to going into business with the Camdens in any way.

But talking to Clair had confirmed what Heddy had known herself—this business was failing fast. She had to make a living. And she couldn't return to nursing to do it. She just couldn't. So where did that leave her?

"My recipes would have to stay a closely guarded secret," she said as if in challenge.

But Lang Camden was unruffled by that, shrugging one broad shoulder. "Sure. We want the finished product, everything else is entirely up to you. But I can help you work out a system where you're the only one who knows the exact ingredients or techniques or whatever it is that you feel will protect your secrets."

The man exuded strength so the idea that he could provide whatever protection she asked for didn't seem beyond his capabilities. Of course he was part of a family she worried she needed protection *from,* but as long as he wasn't asking to have any knowledge or access to her recipes she felt marginally reassured.

"I don't have any money I can invest in this, and I can't—and won't—borrow or go into debt," she warned.

"The money will all come as a grant, free and clear."

"And before I sign anything, my cousin and her husband, who's a lawyer, will have to see it."

"I'm glad you have people you can trust on your side to put your mind to rest. Everything will be up-front and on paper, and we don't have any problem with you showing it to anyone."

Despite his assurances, Heddy was still incredibly nervous about this. She recognized that due to her own family's history with the Camdens, it probably wasn't possible *not* to worry.

But the bottom line was that she didn't feel as if she had another option.

So she heard herself say a very uncertain, "Okay."

But she uttered the word at the exact moment that Carter's lack of coordination with the spoon caused him to shoot a chunk of cheesecake at Lang Camden, splattering it on the front of his well-tailored suit.

"Oh geez, Carter, I just got this back from the cleaner's," Lang complained as he wiped the cheesecake from his lapel with a napkin.

As he focused on that, he missed the fact that Carter, thinking the incident was hilarious, was about to purposely shoot a second glob at him.

Heddy didn't want to get involved but it was clear that disaster was in the offing and if she didn't stop it, no one would.

She reached across the table and took the spoon a split second before Carter could accomplish the next lob. "Uh-uh, we don't throw food," she said firmly.

"Wan-oo," Carter insisted.

"No," Heddy informed him as Lang finally realized what she'd saved him from.

"Hey! No!" he decreed.

"Wan-oo!" Carter responded, plunging a hand into the cheesecake, obviously with every intention of throwing it since Heddy still had his spoon.

Lang grabbed his wrist just in time, shoved the cheesecake plate out of the way and turned his efforts to cleaning Carter's hand rather than his suit coat while Carter launched into a classic terrible-two screaming fit demanding the return of his cheesecake.

Lang apologized over the din.

Heddy got up, went behind her counter, cut a second slice of the blueberry cheesecake and took it back to the table. She set it far out of Carter's reach but because her movements had sparked his curiosity and stopped his screams, she said, "If you can eat it nicely, you can have this other piece."

"Nicey," Carter begrudgingly agreed.

When his hand was clean Heddy slid him the new slice, seeing the toddler rub his eye with his other hand before he dug into the cheesecake.

"Not a good nap today?" Heddy guessed.

"Yeah. No. None at all. I try to get him to take one if I can, but it doesn't usually work out."

"Oh, kids this age have to have a nap," Heddy said. "They need one every day. They need the rest and they need the schedule, the routine..."

She'd said too much. It wasn't her place. She had no idea under what circumstances Lang Camden was car-ing for this child, so she certainly shouldn't be counseling or criticizing.

But he didn't seem to take offense. He just seemed out of his element. Which was strange for someone who seemed so in control otherwise.

"Yeah, there's a lot I have to work out," he said. "I'm learning on the job."

That still didn't tell Heddy who Lang and Carter were to each other and why the man was even attempting to take care of the toddler.

But he didn't satisfy her curiosity. Instead he merely said, "I should probably warn you that until I can get this kid thing squared away and find some help, we're a package deal. He'll be tagging along on everything you and I will need to do."

The thought of seeing the little boy every time she had anything to do with Lang Camden was so painful that Heddy was tempted to say no to the business proposition altogether.

"A package deal?" she queried.

"Where I am, he is these days," Lang answered, pinning her once more with those eyes that seemed like the bluest eyes in the world before he returned to talking business. "Was that an *okay* I heard from you just before the cheesecake attack?"

Heddy offered herself the opportunity to deny it, to not go through with this, after all.

But nothing in her situation had changed in the past several minutes so she said another less-than-enthusiastic, "Yeah."

"Great! You won't be sorry."

Heddy could only hope that proved true.

"So what now?" she asked.

"I'll leave it up to you when to formally close your doors, but my advice is to do it right away. We'll be busy getting this ball rolling so you won't really have time to be here to run this place."

And there was no sense spending any more money on a sinking ship, Heddy thought, assuming he was also thinking that but was being kind enough not to say it.

"I'll have a sign made that announces that your cheesecakes will soon be available at Camden Superstores. You can put it out front. It'll be our first advertisement and then any of your regular customers will know where to look for them in the future."

Heddy nodded, feeling sad at the thought of closing the shop. Then she realized that she felt a little relieved, too, especially knowing that she had something else to move on to.

"For right now," he continued, "let me work up a game plan to get things going the quickest way possible, so you won't have too much downtime between the shop and the new production."

"That would be good," Heddy said, thinking of her already stressed finances.

"I'll do that tonight and tomorrow, then how about if you do a tasting for me tomorrow night? Give me a chance to have a bite of most of the flavors you make—not necessarily the seasonals, but the everyday varieties. We won't want to start out with too many choices. We'll want to introduce some basics, then add to them, maybe do weekly or monthly specials. But let me try nearly everything to see what we want to launch with.

And while I'm gorging on cheesecake we'll go over the game plan I come up with between now and then."

"And paperwork..." Heddy said, still feeling insecure about this whole thing.

"I'll have that drawn up, too. Though I won't have that ready for a couple of days. I'll lay out the grant portion of the deal, and also our standard contract for you to sell cheesecakes to Camden Inc. as soon as you're in production."

"Okay," Heddy repeated, feeling as out of her element in this as he seemed to be with Carter.

Carter, who had finished the second slice of cheesecake and was now nodding off in his chair.

Lang noticed him at the same time Heddy did and used another napkin to wipe the drowsy child's face and hands as he said in a quieter tone, "Looks like you're right. He's tired. I'll get him out of here and maybe he'll snooze a little in the car."

The mother in Heddy wanted to reiterate that Carter needed more than a snooze in the car, but she fought the urge the same way she fought not to like his more intimate tone of voice.

Carter didn't rally much even through his face and hand cleaning. So when the big man stood, he picked up the child and slung him onto one hip.

Sound asleep, Carter's head dropped to Lang's shoulder.

And there was something much too appealing in the sight of them together like that.

Heddy averted her eyes and busied herself gathering dishes.

But then Lang said, "I'm sorry I can't make it tomorrow during business hours. Is it all right that we do the tasting in the evening?"

It seemed rude not to look at him again, not to go with him to the door, so Heddy did. "It's fine. My evenings are not jam-packed. And it will give me the chance during the day to make a few more cheesecake variations for you to taste."

"What time works for you?" he asked, pushing the door open with the same arm that was holding Carter.

"Any time. Work around Carter's dinner. And bedtime..." She was not only thinking of the little boy but doing some fishing as she wondered if Lang had responsibility for the child in the evenings, too.

"Let's say six-thirty. I can usually get him some dinner by then and we should have a pretty decent couple of hours before I'll need to get him home to bed."

So he *did* have the child round-the-clock.

"Six-thirty is fine."

"I guess we're in business," he concluded, holding out his hand for her to shake.

Heddy took it and was instantly more aware than she wanted to be of every sensation of that handshake—of the pure size of his big, masculine hand. Of the warmth and power. Of the confidence.

Of how much she liked the feel of his skin against hers...

The handshake that sealed their business deal ended, and she swallowed back the very unbusinesslike feelings it had prompted in her.

"Six-thirty," she repeated in a voice softer than she wanted it to be.

"Right," he confirmed. "Tomorrow night. See you then."

Heddy merely nodded and watched Lang carry the sleeping child out to his SUV.

As she did, devouring the view, her gaze riveted to the man she was about to see much more of, she realized that somewhere deep down, on a level that was purely instinctive and primitive and absolutely out of her control, she might be experiencing an attraction to him.

An attraction she didn't want to have.

An attraction she *couldn't* have, especially not now that she was in the same position with him that her mother had been with his father once upon a time.

Then, as if to save her from herself, her mind flashed her a painful memory.

A memory of watching Daniel carry Tina the same way Lang Camden was carrying Carter.

That helped offset the attraction.

At least a little anyway.

## *Chapter Three*

"Don't do this, Heddy! You don't know what you're getting into. The Camdens will chew you up and spit you out, just like they did your grandfather and me. Especially me!"

"This ship is already down, Mom. I don't have anything else to lose," Heddy told her mother on Thursday afternoon. As expected, Kitty Hanrahan was horrified by the thought of the venture with the Camdens.

"I talked to Grandpa on the phone this morning and told him," Heddy went on as she put together some of the cheesecakes she wanted Lang Camden to taste in flavors that she didn't already have made or frozen.

Her mother stood nearby watching. "Your grandfather doesn't blame the Camdens the way I do."

"He said it was his own fault for getting in deeper than he should have, for not anticipating that he would need to expand to meet demand."

"And is he forgetting that when we asked for help expanding after the Camdens led us to believe they would give it, they ended up refusing and still took their business away and left us with nothing?"

Heddy had heard it all before and knew that her mother and her grandfather didn't completely agree. But she chose not to argue. Instead, she laid out for her mother why she hoped this was a safer situation.

"The grant money and Lang Camden's expertise will put me in a position to meet demand from the start," she noted. "And if my cheesecakes aren't a success at the Camden stores, I'll still be the owner of the facility and the equipment, so I'll have mass-production capabilities that I don't have now. That will open other avenues I can pursue if I end up needing to."

"Unless the Camdens blacklist you so no one else will ever touch your cheesecakes. You don't know what you're dealing with. I know how Camden men operate—they're good-looking and they reek of charisma, and before you know what's hit you, you're sucked in and then left in their dust."

"I know that's what happened to you—"

"And why Mitchum Camden refused us any help to expand to meet the demands of his stores. When he was finished with me he wanted to forget I existed and the best way to do that was to take his business elsewhere. He didn't care that he was taking away our livelihood."

Heddy didn't know if that was true or not but she did know that that was how her mother had always interpreted what had happened. And even though Heddy's grandfather tried to take the blame for their business failure, he also never explicitly denied Kitty's claims, which lent some credence to them.

Still…

"Grandpa said—and I agree—that I can learn from the past mistakes," Heddy insisted. "And you've just made a good point. I'll make sure that Clark puts some sort of contingency or gag order in the contract I sign with the Camdens so that they *can't* blacklist me or bad-mouth me in any way if things don't work out with them. And Lang Camden has already offered to help me branch into other areas if the cheesecakes don't do well in his stores."

"Don't believe what they say," her mother warned ominously. "Mitchum Camden made me plenty of promises that he didn't keep. Like the engagement ring that ended up on someone else's finger."

"I know," Heddy said sympathetically. "But for me this will be strictly business. I'll make sure everything is on paper, that there aren't any loopholes, and that I'm protected in every way possible. And you don't need to worry about me getting personally involved because that's not going to happen, not with a Camden or any other man. It can't. One man, one marriage, that was it for me—you know that."

"Oh, Heddy…" Her mother's tone was so sad that Heddy knew she'd switched gears even before she said, "I don't want you to go anywhere near a Camden, but I wish you *would* get involved with *someone* again. Five years is a long time—long enough to grieve. I don't want to see you alone forever."

"I'm okay," Heddy assured her. "I'm not grieving anymore. Honestly. And I'm happy enough." As happy as she could be now and could hope to be later. "But Daniel was my one-and-only and I can't even imagine myself with anyone else. Or having any more kids—"

"You would have had at least one more baby if what happened hadn't happened," her mother pointed out.

"But now every kid makes me think of Tina—" Ache for Tina… "—and the only way to avoid that is to stay away from kids. Another baby would have been a brother or a sister for Tina. It would have made a full, complete family. Now having another child would be like I was trying to replace Tina somehow. As if that could ever be done. So no, the whole marriage and kids thing is just a part of life that's over for me. And I'm okay with it. Daniel was my husband. Tina was my little girl. No one else can ever fill those slots."

Not even the handsome, charming, sexy Lang Camden or the very cute Carter who both sprang to mind suddenly for no reason Heddy understood.

"Getting involved with someone is just not on the menu for me," she concluded firmly. "So there's no risk of *that* part of your history repeating itself. And I think I can protect myself from the rest of it happening again."

"I still don't like it," Kitty said. "None of it. Your involvement with the Camdens and your refusal to go on living your life."

"I'm *living* just fine," Heddy said with a laugh at her mother's dramatics.

"You're not, Heddy. You're not…"

"I'm going to be a big cheesecake mogul, Mom. That's living, phase two—successful career woman."

Her mother was standing beside her, near enough to

pull her head to the side and kiss the top of it. "It's not enough," her mother whispered.

But Heddy insisted that it was.

And again shooed away the mental image of Lang Camden that almost seemed to make her mother's case.

"What exactly is a start-up guy?" Heddy asked Lang that evening, hoping to find out more about what he did for Camden Incorporated.

He and Carter had arrived on time for the tasting but Carter had again been overly tired and cranky. Lang hadn't come equipped with any diversions for the child, so Heddy stepped in and gave him pots and pans and wooden spoons to play with. But it had quickly become clear that the little boy was just too tired to be appeased.

So, at Heddy's suggestion, they'd moved the tasting from the shop to her living area in the back where she'd persuaded Carter to lie on her comfy couch with a pillow and a fluffy blanket. She'd found a children's station on television for him to watch, and he'd promptly fallen asleep.

She and Lang sat alone at her round pedestal kitchen table while he methodically sampled the array of cheesecake flavors she'd set out for him. Without the distraction of Carter, Heddy felt the need to make conversation. Lang's comments about which of the cheesecakes he thought they should start with and which should be featured later weren't enough.

Plus she was curious about him.

She hated that she was. But she was.

"The brandy mousse—wonderful but tastes seasonal. Let's hold off and do that as a Christmas or New Year's flavor," he said, waiting for Heddy to make a note before he answered her question. "What do I do as the start-up guy? Well, when the decision gets made to open a new store or to branch out, the first thing I do is the research. If it's a new store, I start by doing the demographics and scouting for the best location. From there I do all the groundwork, bid on the land, deal with zoning, apply for the permits, find contractors.... Things that set the wheels into motion."

"And if it's a new endeavor?"

"I do what I'll be doing with you. If we want to add a department or to start selling something we haven't sold before, I look for the best way to do that. Is it better to buy from someone else who produces what we want to sell? If so, under what terms, and can they supply to the extent we need? Or, is it better if we set up production ourselves? If it is, I look for facilities and for the best people to man the operation, and I get it going."

"My situation is a combination of those. You're doing what you'd ordinarily do to set up your own production, except that you're doing it for me."

"Yeah," he confirmed.

"And if you decide along the way that you'd be better off producing your own cheesecakes?" Heddy asked.

Things were more casual tonight. She was in jeans and a plain blouse she wore untucked. He was in tweed slacks and a sport shirt. And yet even sitting in her spotless white kitchen with its bright red and navy blue accents, separated from her cozy living room and Carter only by an island counter, it was still in the back of Heddy's mind to find the pitfalls in this deal.

"Not going to happen," he said without any indication that he'd taken offense at her suspicion. "You make the best cheesecakes and you have the recipes and the techniques. I already told you that I'm fine with you guarding those things. I'm not trying to wiggle my way in and steal your trade secrets so we can turn around and produce the cheesecakes ourselves."

Heddy had no idea why the thought of him *wiggling his way in* to anything seemed a tad alluring but she ignored it and forced herself to focus on more important matters.

"But even as it is—just tonight—you're learning things you could copy. Flavor combinations I put together. Brainstorms I've had for varieties no one else makes—"

"Anybody who walked into your shop and tasted something would have that same information, wouldn't they?"

Heddy shrugged, conceding his point. She had been fairly revealing in telling him how she got certain degrees of flavor—for instance in her blackberry chocolate cheesecake—and now she wished she hadn't.

"Think of the big picture, Heddy," he advised. "With some things it's to our advantage to go into production ourselves—to have our own factories—because it would cost us more to buy from someone else. But for this? For one item in a line of gourmet foods? That's a niche. It's more cost- and time-efficient to buy what you produce than to find and hire chefs to develop a recipe, to have to continue to operate production after it's set up, to have the expense of employees, their benefits and what-have-you long-term. Just for cheesecakes. Can't you see that it makes more sense to do it this way? We're not conspiring against you. We're just doing good business that will hopefully benefit us all."

Heddy did see that perspective and decided that, if she was going to do this, she needed to tune out some of her mother's concerns.

"So that's what I do as Camden Superstores' start-up guy," Lang concluded. "What about you? Have you always been a cheesecake maker? Were you baking for someone else and then decided to go out on your own or—"

Heddy shook her head. "Before the shop I just made cheesecakes for fun. It was one of those things where every time somebody ate one they'd tell me I should go into business. So when I needed a change of paths, I thought I'd give it a try."

"It's just not so easy to make a living even when what you're selling *is* this good," he concluded.

"I guess not."

"What did you need a change of path from?" he asked, taking his third bite of the blackberry chocolate cheesecake even though the decision had already been made to use it as one of the first flavors.

"I was a pediatric nurse. I worked at Children's Hospital."

"Sick kids… I'd guess there's a pretty high burnout rate in that," he said.

"It wasn't burnout."

"You left for another reason?" he queried.

She caught herself staring at the bit of scruffy beard that shadowed his sculpted jaw and registering how much she liked it. In an effort to stop studying the man, she rearranged the plates so some of the samples he'd yet to taste were closer to him.

"Something happened that changed my whole life," she admitted. "Overnight. For a while I couldn't even get out of bed in the morning. Then, when I had to, I just couldn't go back to what I'd been doing before. I needed something different."

She didn't know why she'd even told him that much.

Maybe it was the soft way those blue eyes were now looking at her. They just sort of sucked her in....

He nodded. "Sometimes life kicks you in the teeth," he said as if he understood even without knowing any of the details.

"Sometimes it does," she agreed. "Did life kick you in the teeth and leave you with Carter?" she asked, knowing she was prying and that it was probably out of line. But she didn't want to go on talking about herself and she couldn't help wondering.

"It's more like a kick in the teeth spun me around in a direction I shouldn't have taken and Carter is what came out of that."

Heddy's confusion must have shown in her expression because he laughed. And then he surprised her with his candidness.

"I spun out of one relationship into a rebound..." He searched for the right word, then said, "I don't know if you could call it a rebound *relationship* exactly, because the whole thing was purely physical. And safe, I thought. But whatever you call it, I spun out of one relationship that actually *was* a relationship and got involved with someone else. For just a little while before it got weird."

"Weird?"

"You know how those things go. I met this woman named Viv at a party. She seemed normal. Really, really cheery, but normal. We hit it off, started seeing each other—"

"On a purely physical basis," Heddy reminded him, unsure exactly why that made her feel something and what that something was. It couldn't have been jealousy....

"It was purely physical," he confirmed. "But it barely lasted a few weeks before she sort of freaked out on me. I found out after the fact, from a friend of hers, that she had some pretty severe emotional and mental problems. Apparently we met in one of her *up* times—that accounted for the cheeriness. She was happy, full of energy, fun. But then she crashed...."

"Not so much fun."

"Definitely not. In fact she was a little scary. The woman had a really dark *down* side. I tried to convince her to get help, but that was a hot-button issue. About the time *I* was getting freaked out and wondering what I'd gotten myself into, she had one of her wild, irrational outbursts and said she didn't want to ever see me again. I figured I'd dodged a bullet and was only too happy to call it quits."

"Then she wanted it on again?"

"No, that was it. The last I ever saw or heard from her. A little over three years ago. I wrote it off to a bad dating experience and forgot about it. Until the end of January when I got a call from social services...."

He said that ominously.

"Surprise, you're a daddy?" Heddy offered on a guess.

"Not quite. They said they had this kid—sadly neglected, abandoned by his mother with a note saying she didn't know which of four men his father was."

*"Four?"*

"Yeah. Like I said, I was rebounding, spinning, I didn't actually ask if she was seeing someone else."

"And she was seeing *three* someone elses?"

"That's what the social worker said. That there were four candidates for Carter's father and I was one of them."

"Oh, dear."

"Yeah," he said, grimacing and showing that he wasn't proud of any of what he was telling her. Which somehow made her appreciate that he *was* telling her.

"Anyway, Viv had made it clear that she wanted nothing more to do with being a mother. She'd relinquished all parental rights. But DNA testing was necessary to determine the kid's father. Then whoever it was could either take him or relinquish their rights, too, so he could be adopted and not just left to be shuffled through foster care his whole life. I jumped at DNA testing because I was so sure the kid couldn't be mine. I was really careful."

"But things fail..." Another guess.

"Apparently so. No one was more shocked than I was when the test proved Carter was mine."

"And rather than signing away your parental rights for someone else to raise him, you took him."

Lang's eyebrows arched toward his hairline as he closed his eyes and breathed a sigh. "He's my flesh and blood. I couldn't... I had to... You know..."

Obviously it hadn't been an easy decision. Or one he was finding easy to live with.

"I didn't—pretty much *don't*—know the first thing about kids," he said with a self-deprecating laugh, adding facetiously, "You probably didn't even notice, did you?"

Heddy merely smiled, not wanting to criticize.

"But yeah, he's mine and I took him. Only I kind of dropped the ball after catching it," he confided, his expression showing guilt now.

"How so?"

"I've been passing him around to my two sisters, my cousin Jani and my grandmother—the women in my family. They've really been doing the work. I just sort of drove him from one of their places to the other."

Heddy laughed. "Good plan."

"Yeah, but last weekend that came to an end. They ganged up on me and said it was time for me to step up to the plate. That I was on my own with Carter. They gave me a crash course in how to take care of him, made sure I could do it all with at least some proficiency, and that was it. I left the family's weekly Sunday dinner at my grandmother's house with Carter, a boatload of instructions and no more help."

"None?"

"None," he said in a dire tone. "I have my secretary interviewing nannies, but so far that hasn't gone anywhere. Although I'm fairly certain that she's under orders from my grandmother to take her time. And until I get some help, Carter is all mine, day and night."

"Why would your grandmother give your secretary orders to be slow about finding you a nanny?"

"She thinks Carter and I need to get to know each other without anyone running interference, that we have to 'bond,'" he said, clearly repeating the term someone else had used. "My family has come up with some theories about me since the kick-in-the-teeth—their armchair psychoanalysis—and they think the only way I'll ever actually let Carter in and *become* a father to him is if I don't have any kind of buffer."

"You don't agree?"

He shrugged. "I don't know. Seems to me that if this was a normal situation there would be two parents so there would be some built-in buffers and support, wouldn't there? But like I said, I don't know anything about parenthood or about bonding or any of that. I'm just doing the best I can right now. It's all new to me. Carter is new to me. I'm new to him. We're finding our way, I guess. I hope. All I know without a doubt is that I might be the Camden Superstores start-up guy, but I'm not doing so well as a start-up dad. *Dad.* Even saying the word feels strange."

"Look on the bright side. You're past the bottles and the middle-of-the-night feedings, the colic, the teaching to eat solid foods, the teething, the crying for no reason for hours on end, the endless pacing and jiggling and bouncing to try to stop that crying...."

"You know a lot about this stuff."

Heddy merely shrugged. "I'm just saying you could have even more on your hands."

"Seems like most days I still have quite a bit on my hands.... And down the front of my clothes, and in my face, and on my shoes, and in my hair or his and—"

"It will get better," Heddy assured him with another laugh.

"Easy for you to say."

Actually, none of this was easy for her to talk about. But Heddy didn't tell him that she would give anything to be where he was with her own daughter, to have been able to know Tina at two and a half....

"My family probably *is* right," he admitted. "Carter is mine. It's not just a matter of paying the bills or pushing him off on other people to take care of. And I don't want him to grow up without ever getting to know him, without him ever knowing me. I want to be good at this. I'm just having a tough time coming to grips with instant fatherhood to a two-and-a-half-year-old. I figured I'd have kids *someday.* Just not like this...."

"The things that aren't *supposed* to happen are the hardest to accept," Heddy agreed, realizing that in sharing some personal information and letting her see a little vulnerability, Lang Camden was all the more appealing.

Which meant that they should get back to strictly business.

"Last one," she said, pushing forward the slice of chocolate orange spice cheesecake.

Lang tasted it, savored it and showed his appreciation with a rapturous roll of the eyes.

He swallowed and said, "Lady, you really know what you're doing with cheesecake. I can't believe you haven't had customers lined up outside your door."

"Since you'll be selling the cheesecakes, I'm glad you feel that way."

"Write up a bill for all of these. Let's pack the leftovers, and I'll take them with me. Will they keep until Sunday?"

Heddy hadn't thought he would pay her for this but in her financial situation she couldn't afford to argue. "Wrapped well and refrigerated, yes, they'll still be good on Sunday. Or you could freeze them and they'd last longer than that."

"Sunday will be fine. We have family dinner every Sunday at my grandmother's house. We all bring something and I think fifteen of these cheesecakes *might* be enough," he said.

"They're small," Heddy warned. She'd used her six-inch pans to make the samples.

"Then you better throw in whatever you have left in the case today that will still be good on Sunday because there are a lot of us."

Heddy wasn't sure if he was doing this as a way of reimbursing her for what would otherwise be a loss or if he genuinely wanted the cheesecakes for his Sunday dinner. But again, she didn't argue. She only said, "I hope you have a big refrigerator."

"Big and mostly empty. I'm not much of a cook."

Heddy was pleasantly surprised by the fact that he pitched in and worked right alongside her to wrap and box all the cheesecakes. Then, while Carter was still sleeping on her sofa, she helped Lang load them into the rear portion of his SUV.

After he wrote her a substantial check for the cheesecakes and left it on the table, Heddy found herself standing not far in front of him in her kitchen, looking up into that handsome face as he said, "So, we're on for Saturday? We'll look at what commercial kitchen space is for sale and hit the restaurant supply store to get started ordering some basic equipment—mixers, pans, that kind of thing? On my dime for now, to come out of the grant when the paperwork is finished, of course. Which should be early next week."

"I'm all yours."

It was just an expression. But it had come out wrong.

He grinned as if the idea intrigued him, and with a hint of flirtatious wickedness said, "Great."

"What time on Saturday?" Heddy asked, trying to put things back on the business track.

"I can pick you up at ten. How's that?"

"If you tell me where, I can just meet you."

He shook his head. "We'll be traveling from one space to another, then to the supply store. Why caravan when I can just pick you up? The car seat is in my backseat, so it isn't as if my passenger side is occupied. No reason to have two cars."

Except that it was slightly disturbing for Heddy to think of riding like that with him and Carter, like a family of three out on a Saturday excursion together. The way she and Daniel and Tina had spent many a Saturday…

But what was she going to say? He was right—it didn't make sense for them to be driving separately.

"Okay," she agreed.

But apparently he saw her hesitation because he smiled an endearing smile and said, "Don't you trust my driving? Because I can hire a car and driver if you're worried."

The image of a chauffeured limousine taking them

around town to look at kitchen space was too silly not to make Heddy smile in spite of herself.

"Well, that is the way I usually travel, but I suppose I can adapt—if I must," she joked.

"I wouldn't want to cramp your style."

"It's okay, just this once I'll leave my diamonds and furs at home, I'll give up the limo and you can be my driver."

His supple mouth stretched into a grin that was too brilliant, too engaging, too delighted for her focus not to just naturally go there.

And when it did, the next thought that sauntered through her mind was an image of what it might be like if he leaned in, bent over just a little and pressed those lips to hers....

Heddy didn't know where that had come from but she was grateful when Lang said, "At your service," and the sound of his deep, deep voice helped drag her to her senses.

*I'm never going to kiss this man!* she mentally shouted at herself. She didn't *want* to kiss this man. She didn't want to kiss any man who wasn't Daniel, and certainly not a Camden.

She'd just lost her mind for a minute.

Luckily it seemed as though he couldn't read it, because he turned away from her then and crossed to Carter.

"If you want, you can just wrap the blanket around him and strap him into his car seat like that, rather than getting him into his coat," Heddy offered. "He might be more likely to stay sleeping."

"Thanks. I'll bring the blanket back on Saturday."

Heddy walked with them through her shop and held the door open for Lang as he carried the slumbering child out, then followed them to the SUV and opened the back door.

Lang secured Carter in his car seat and Heddy couldn't resist reaching in to pull the blanket over one of the child's shoulders before they both stepped out of the way and Lang closed the car door.

"See? Things go more smoothly with help, details all get taken care of," Lang said, possibly referring to their earlier conversation about how he was now on his own in parenting Carter.

"But you *could* have done without it. You would have been fine," Heddy pointed out.

"Thanks just the same," he said, looking down at her much the way he had been in the kitchen when the idea of kissing him had sprung into her head, his blue eyes just too, too appealing.

"Go in, it's cold," he ordered, poking his chiseled chin in the direction of her house as he opened his car door. "I'll see you Saturday morning."

"At ten. I'll be ready," Heddy reiterated, doing as she'd been told and leaving him to go inside.

But as she turned to close the door behind her, she saw that Lang was still standing where she'd left him, with his car door open. Watching her.

And seeming lost for that moment in thoughts of his own.

She didn't for a minute believe that he was thinking what she'd been thinking. That he was thinking about kissing her.

And yet, she was shocked at herself when it occurred to her that somewhere deep down she might have liked it—just a little—if he was.

## *Chapter Four*

Saturday was a long day for Carter. Heddy and Lang dragged him around to meet with Lang's Realtor to look at commercial kitchen space for sale.

It would have been a long day for Heddy, too, except not only was she interested in the spaces and what she would be using them for, she liked watching Lang Camden in action.

Actually she just liked watching Lang Camden, period.

Dressed in jeans that hugged his hips, thighs and a remarkable rear end, a royal blue field sweater and a leather jacket that looked as soft as butter, he was certainly something to look at.

But he was also a business presence to be reckoned with. He was knowledgeable, observant, informed and so just plain smart that nothing got past him. When it came to finding her the best space, talking about running a business out of it and getting a fair price, the man knew his stuff, and it was impressive.

It was also impressive how down-to-earth he was in the process. There was nothing dictatorial about him, nothing tyrannical or elitist or entitled. He valued both Heddy's opinions and those of the Realtor. He listened to Heddy's concerns when she had them. He asked for her viewpoint at every stage and kept her needs and desires at the forefront.

And he ultimately found her an ideal space that was halfway between Arcada and Denver—both convenient for her commute and a prime spot for deliveries to go in and out. Then he made it clear to the Realtor that the place would be paid for from a grant from the Camdens, but that Heddy would be the owner, free and clear.

What Lang wasn't so impressive at was managing Carter in the meantime. In fact, Lang was mostly oblivious to the little boy and while the adults looked at the spaces, he found various ways to entertain himself.

He ran races, crashing into the wall to stop, then turning to race to the opposite wall.

He spun around bare support poles until he fell down dizzy.

He kicked a soda can he found in one space, clattering it endlessly until Heddy took it away from him so they didn't have to shout over the din.

And at another site he decided to entertain himself by trying to insert a stick into an electrical outlet. Luckily Heddy had spotted him before he actually did it, averting disaster.

But it *was* Heddy who was on the lookout for that disaster and who stepped in to keep it from happening.

It was Heddy who'd had to put a stop to Carter's races and pole-spinning, while Lang seemed completely surprised by the need for such interventions. In business, nothing got by him, but as a start-up dad, he was in over his head.

They found a space that Heddy and Lang agreed was perfect, so Lang suggested they make an offer. The Realtor then spent time on the phone, came back with a verbal acceptance from the owner and wanted papers signed. All of that had taken a while and since Lang had also made an appointment for them to meet with a sales representative at a supply store at the end of the day, there was no time for Carter to nap.

By then Carter was obviously weary, and after Lang finally did register that the child shouldn't be using a wooden spoon as a drum stick to bang against bowls and stopped it, a weary and pouty Carter climbed into a giant soup pot and curled up as if he was in need of a refuge.

Heddy had been trying not to be drawn in by the little boy, to do nothing more than she needed to do to keep him safe and to keep the noise level at a minimum. But seeing the tiny child collapse in a soup pot made her feel bad for him. She couldn't keep herself from lifting him out and setting him on her lap to rest while she and Lang talked with the sales rep at his desk.

And when the child laid his head against her and fell asleep, it left her fluctuating between a sense of warm satisfaction and a dull ache of longing for her own baby.

It was after six o'clock by the time Heddy and Lang left the supply store with a lengthy list of items to get her started and a substantial price estimate.

As Lang drove back to Heddy's place he talked about getting bids from other supply stores now that they had a list to work from, but Heddy was only partially paying attention.

The day was coming to a close and she was reluctant to let that happen.

If she merely had Lang drop her off—the way she *should*—she would be going into her dark, silent house to spend another Saturday night alone.

After five years of that she should have been used to it, but somehow she still hated Saturday nights and Sundays the most.

And for some reason tonight, she was even more loath to face it.

But what she *could* do was ask Lang and Carter to come in....

There wasn't a doubt in her mind that she was in dangerous territory. That she could be crossing the line between business and personal. The line she knew she shouldn't go anywhere near—let alone cross—with Lang Camden.

But it was Saturday night.

She was a bundle of excitement and nerves over this new business venture and she just didn't want to go into her too quiet house and be alone from now until whenever.

Besides, all any of them had had to eat today was a greasy, insubstantial fast-food lunch, and there was a part of Heddy—the maternal part—that wanted to feed Carter a good meal.

"Do you have plans for dinner?" she heard herself

ask as he pulled into her driveway and stopped in the small gravel parking lot beside the house.

"Let's see..." Lang mused facetiously. "I usually grab a pizza or burger from somewhere on the way home. Does that count as a plan?"

"Mmm, sort of, I guess," Heddy hedged. "I was just thinking that I have all the makings for a chicken pot-pie, if you're interested. After all you've done today—"

"You don't have to feed us," he said in a tone that also said he was open to the suggestion.

"How about if I just do it for the heck of it?"

"Really? I'd love that," Lang said without any more hesitation. "I'll even pitch in. As kids we all had to help fix dinner every night, so there are a few things I can do around a kitchen. Do you need me to run to the store for anything? How about wine?"

Wine?

That got her closer to crossing the line.

And yet despite telling herself to decline the offer, she quipped, "Carter can't have wine."

"You and I can, though, can't we? White to go with chicken?"

"I like white wine," Heddy said as if she were only imparting information. Not crossing any lines.

"Great. Shall we all just go or do you want to go inside and get dinner started while Carter and I get the wine?"

Thinking it would buy her a little time to spruce up after her long day, Heddy said, "Why don't you and Carter go and I'll get started in the kitchen? There's a liquor store in the strip mall straight down the street, about six blocks, you can't miss it." She pointed out the direction he needed to go before she opened the passenger door and climbed out. "I'll see you guys in a few minutes."

"Guys," Carter said from his car seat, making his presence known, reminding her that having him there kept things from getting too personal between her and Lang because Carter almost acted as a chaperone.

"When you get back, if you pull around behind the house, that's where I park. You can come in the kitchen door and that way it won't look like I'm open for business again."

"Got it," he confirmed just before Heddy closed the door, waved to Carter and went up to her house.

Trying, as she did, to ignore the fact that her heart was beating fast and that she was suddenly looking forward to *this* Saturday night more than any she could remember in the past five years.

After rushing upstairs to her bedroom and making sure her jeans and the lightweight white turtleneck sweater she had on were still presentable, she brushed on a little fresh blush, applied another swipe of mascara and some lip gloss.

She decided her hair needed a little more attention though.

She'd put it in a French twist this morning to look professional, but apparently had rolled it more snugly than she should have because it had begun to feel as if it were giving her a face-lift.

She told herself that undoing it was merely to give herself some relief. That it had nothing to do with looking more casual for her Saturday evening of entertaining.

But she still took extra pains brushing it before pulling it into a very loose knot at her nape that left it puffy and a bit come-hither.

Maybe she *should* put it back in another French twist, she thought when she noticed the effect. Certainly she didn't want to send the wrong message.

But it felt so much better not to have the tug of the French twist, she ended up leaving it. Anyway, she needed to cook, not spend more time on her appearance, so she went downstairs to the kitchen.

Making pastry crust and gathering the ingredients for the potpie occupied the remainder of the time until Lang and Carter returned.

Impressed that Lang washed his hands and Carter's before helping in the kitchen, she set him to chopping vegetables while she made the gravy for the potpie.

She was also surprised that Lang actually showed a knack for engaging Carter's help in the kitchen, too.

"I think you know your way around cooking more than you let on," she said as she watched him have Carter move thinly sliced carrots from the cutting board into the bowl waiting for the vegetables.

"I was six when we all went to live with my grandmother. She had household help—Margaret and Louie—but dinners were up to GiGi."

"The cook?"

He laughed. "There was no *cook.* GiGi is what we call my grandmother. Anyway, fixing dinner was always up to GiGi and the ten of us kids. GiGi was very big on our having that time as a family together. I can't say I actually know any recipes, but I take instruction in the kitchen well because I had training in that."

This raised a number of questions in Heddy's mind. But rather than going off on several different paths to understand how he—and nine other *kids*—had come to live with the grandmother they called GiGi, she stuck with the subject at hand.

"Is that how you know what to do to keep Carter busy now—from your own experience as a kid in the kitchen?" Because he seemed clueless about doing anything to occupy the child the rest of the time.

"I guess so," he mused as if that hadn't occurred to him.

Then, before Heddy could ask any more questions, he finished chopping the vegetables, gave them to Heddy for sautéing and suggested that he and Carter set the table while Heddy put the potpie in the oven and made the salad.

As she mixed greens and added apples and mandarin oranges in the hope of enticing Carter to eat the salad—and dressed it with a balsamic vinegar, also with Carter in mind—she watched Lang patiently instruct the little boy in the proper way to set a table, including folding the paper napkins.

Again she marveled at the man. He might be a rookie parent, but seeing how well he was doing with the child made Heddy believe that his family might have been right to force him into caregiving. That he really was capable of being a good dad to Carter when he actually put his mind to it.

Heddy filled the water glasses to go with the wine she and Lang were having, and took the potpie out of the oven. As Heddy brought the food to the table, Lang used an enormous dictionary he found in Heddy's bookcase as a booster seat for Carter so he could better reach the table. Heddy suggested tying a towel around the little boy's middle and the back of the chair to steady him so he didn't tumble to the floor. After that was done they all sat down to eat.

Heddy had apparently been right about Carter needing a home-cooked meal because he ate heartily of the potpie—vegetables and all—and even of the salad, though he ate more of the fruit than the greens.

But he really did have a sweet tooth because when she brought out a plate of brownies, he ate one, stole a second, and would have had a third had Lang not caught him before he could snatch it.

After a quick, wiggly cleanup, Carter was released from the towel tie. At that point he requested cartoons, so Heddy again set him up on the couch with the blanket Lang had returned, a pillow and the television tuned to the cartoon channel. Within about ten minutes the toddler was sound asleep again, leaving Heddy and Lang to do the dishes—something Lang insisted he help with.

"So tell me about the Hanrahans," Lang said as they cleared the table. "And how come your last name is Hanrahan? I know the bread bakery all those years ago was Hanrahans Bakery, and that it belonged to your mom's father, right?"

"Right."

"Which would make your mom's maiden name Hanrahan."

"Right, she's Kitty—short for Katherine—Hanrahan."

"So does the fact that you have her maiden name mean that you didn't have a dad in the picture?" Lang asked tentatively.

Heddy laughed. "No, my dad was, and is, in the picture. He's Jim Craig, happily married to my mom for the last thirty-five years."

"Kitty *Hanrahan*."

"Right. My grandfather was an only child so he was all there was to carry on the Hanrahan name. Then he had three daughters. He hated the thought that his name would die with him. My aunts took their husbands' last names when they married, but for my grandfather's sake my mom decided to keep Hanrahan even after marrying my dad. Since I have an older brother—who was already carrying on the Craig name, my mom talked my dad into letting me be a Hanrahan, too."

"Ah, I see. And when you get married?"

"I already did that and stayed Hanrahan," Heddy said softly. And Tina had been Tina Hanrahan, the hope being that there would be a son who could take the Doyle name. All to make Heddy's grandfather feel as if his name still had a chance to survive. Which, now, it wouldn't…

"You were married?" Lang asked cautiously.

But that wasn't something she was ready to talk about with him. "I thought you wanted to know about the Hanrahans."

The dishes were all in the dishwasher by then and after tidying up the rest of the kitchen, Heddy had come to stand in the bend behind the L-shaped counter. She was leaning against the edge, facing Lang, who raised his chin as if to confirm that he got the message that she didn't want to talk about her marriage.

"Okay, the Hanrahans."

"There are my grandparents—still living. My parents. Me. And my older brother, Max. He's a dentist in New Mexico."

"So your parents are still happily married?" Lang asked, making her wonder again if he was aware of the romance between his father and Kitty and was fishing for information about Kitty.

"They are. Are yours?"

"My parents died in a plane crash when I was six. Along with my aunt and uncle, and my grandfather."

"I'm sorry. I didn't know that," Heddy said somberly. Her entire life she'd heard her mother rail against the Camdens and say what a dirty dog Mitchum Camden was in particular, leaving out no detail of her breakup with Mitchum. But beyond that, Heddy knew nothing about the Camdens.

"That's why you went to live with your grandmother when you were six?" she asked.

"Me, my sisters—we're triplets—and our three brothers and four cousins. Yep, after the plane crash GiGi took us all on."

"I knew you were a big family but I had no idea..."

"Yeah. Ten grandchildren, and GiGi raised us. So how could I be scared of one kid when she took on that many?" He paused a moment before changing the subject. "Your grandparents are both still alive, too. Well and happy and together?"

"They are."

"So after the bakery, your mom and your grandfather came out okay?"

"Well, eventually," Heddy said, unwilling to gloss over the hardships she knew her mother and grandfather had suffered.

"But not right away?" Lang asked as if he needed to know but didn't really want to.

"At first they tried hard to restart the bakery," Heddy said. "To go back to the way it was before their involvement with the Camden stores. There was a fair share of local restaurants and delis that they'd supplied with bread and rolls, and they'd had a decent walk-in business. But the restaurants and delis all had different suppliers by then and wouldn't switch back."

"What about different restaurants and delis?"

"There'd been some bad word of mouth from their old customers, who were mad when they'd bailed on them to bake only for the Camdens. My grandfather tried to get some new clients—and he got a few—but mainly he'd lost trust among the small businesses. They viewed him and my mom as traitors who'd sold out and gotten what they'd deserved when the Camden stores dumped them. They just ran into too many people who thought it was only a matter of time until they hooked another big fish and cut bait on the little guys again."

"And the little guys didn't want to be left in the lurch. They wanted a supplier they knew would be there for them."

"Exactly. Hanrahans had lost any credibility with the small business owners and there was no getting it back."

"And the walk-in business?"

"They'd moved from a location with a good storefront to a larger place in a more industrial area, because they didn't need a storefront. When Camdens pulled their business Grandpa didn't have the money to relocate again and there really wasn't any walk-in business where they were. They sent out fliers. They ran ads. They gave out coupons, put up signs… But nothing brought people out of their way. They just didn't have the business to keep going, so about a year after the split with the Camdens, they had to close up shop."

"And when they did?" Lang asked quietly.

"More rough times."

"Financially?"

"Sure. But in other ways, too."

"'Other ways'?" Lang repeated to prompt her to go on.

Her mother had been emotionally miserable for a long while but Heddy didn't want to talk about that. Instead she only told him about the business portion. "Mom and Grandpa had both had such high hopes. When the rug was pulled out from under them, it was all just…I don't know, so discouraging and depressing and demoralizing for them both. So painful…"

"But they got other jobs," Lang said hopefully, obviously not eager to hear the downside.

But he'd asked and there had been downsides. And while she wasn't yet ready to tell him about the romance between his father and her mother if it was something he was unaware of, she wasn't going to sugarcoat the rest.

"My mom was younger, she went on to a couple of jobs she hated—office work mainly—until she found something else for herself. But the real financial loss was my grandfather's and he felt like a complete failure. He bottomed out for a while—or so I've been told. I wasn't born then and he doesn't like to talk about it."

"What have you been told?"

"That he felt responsible. He felt as if he'd put my mom in harm's way, as if he'd hurt her. He had some debilitating guilt. He's usually an even-tempered, upbeat guy—I've never known him to be any other way. But I guess he went into a really deep funk. He couldn't get a job. He'd sunk everything he had into trying to restart the bakery—including taking a second mortgage on his house, so he nearly lost that."

Lang's eyebrows arched over those incredible blue eyes. "*Did* he lose his house?"

"It was headed to foreclosure but they pulled it out in the end. Only not before my grandmother left him."

"Oh geez, it gets worse...."

"My grandmother leaving him was a rude awakening for my grandfather. He pulled himself together, got a job making bread for a big grocery store chain, then talked my grandmother into coming back to him and managed to save the house. He even says that some good came from all the bad."

"How so?"

"Working for a big chain gave him health insurance that he didn't have before. So when my grandmother needed spinal surgery a year later, she could have the medical care he wouldn't have been able to afford before."

"I guess that is *some* good. How does your grandfather feel about the grant and your new arrangement selling to Camden Superstores? Is he upset about it?"

Lang's worried expression showed what he expected

that answer to be, and Heddy had the urge to smooth her fingertips across his lined brow, to ease away some of the stress she'd put there.

But merely having the urge shocked her and she certainly wasn't going to give in to it.

Besides, she reasoned, she was only telling him the truth. And the answer to that question wasn't what he thought it was going to be. "Actually, my grandfather isn't against it," she told him. "He wants me to be careful, but he thinks that if I don't make the mistakes he made, it could work out. He's wondering if this is guilt-money, though."

"My family is glad to have a second chance to make things work," Lang said without admitting to anything else. Then, looking into her eyes more intently than he had been, he added, "*I'm* glad to have the chance to make this work for *you.* I'm just hoping the past can be the past."

"I'm not carrying a grudge, if that's what you're thinking. And I'm grateful for the opportunity your grant is giving me."

"This really can be a fresh start then?"

"I hope so."

"I know I'll do my damnedest," he promised. Then he smiled a cocky smile and said, "After all, you *are* the premier cheesecake-maker."

"*Premier...* Wow." Heddy appreciated his attempt to lighten the tone.

"Superior, unequaled, incomparable, foremost and best." He went on teasing her with accolades while his blue eyes stayed steady and warm on her.

"You realize that we haven't set the price for them yet, don't you," she goaded.

He grinned. "We'd better just stick with premier then."

His gaze stayed on her as if he liked what he saw and was enjoying himself again. Enjoying being there with her. Heddy realized that if this were a first date, this was the kind of moment when she'd definitely be thinking of accepting a second date with this guy.

And even as part of her brain was reminding her that this *wasn't* a date, and that there wouldn't be any dates in the future, either, another part flipped back to Thursday night when she'd wondered what it might be like to be kissed by Lang.

Except that tonight she wasn't just wondering about it fleetingly the way she had on Thursday. Tonight she found herself tipping her chin upward as if it might actually happen. And doing a little more than wondering about it, fantasizing some, too.

Then he pivoted ever so slightly toward her and she saw his gaze drop to her mouth.

And linger…

It would be so easy for him to just lean forward and kiss her….

And that part of her that she didn't want to own up to wished that he might.

Then he leaned a tiny bit forward as if that was exactly what he was going to do and Heddy panicked.

She stiffened and stood straighter, leaning away from him as she thought fast. "Would you like coffee or tea? Maybe another brownie to go with it? Carter has the couch but we could sit at the kitchen table again."

He knew. Heddy could see in his heart-stoppingly handsome face that he knew she'd thought she was about to be kissed and was fleeing from it.

He stood taller, too, and shook his head. "I'm good. I should probably get Carter home to bed."

But rather than move in the direction of the child he continued to look at Heddy so softly, so warmly. He was being understanding about her panic and merely moving on. "What's on the docket for your Sunday?" he asked.

"The docket for my Sunday… I was thinking that I might try to take down my sign out front. It doesn't light up, so there's no wiring to it or anything, and I can unscrew the sign part. But I don't know about the poles that go down into the ground. Unless you weren't telling the truth about the paperwork coming this week and I *shouldn't* close my doors…"

"Paperwork. This week as promised. And as for the sign, we have people who do things like that. I'll send a crew on Monday. What about Sunday dinner with your family or something?"

"No, we don't do anything like that on a regular basis. We get together for birthdays or anniversaries or just when we feel like it, but there's nothing going on tomorrow."

"*My* family has Sunday dinner every week at GiGi's. It's a very big deal—the whole family comes and brings people."

"Just anyone off the street?" Heddy teased.

"No, friends, family of friends, people they're seeing… My cousin Cade is engaged so his fiancée will be there, along with her grandfather Jonah, who is also

GiGi's former high school sweetheart and current companion. Margaret and Louie are always there."

"The staff?"

"Well, yeah, that's their job description, I guess, but they're there as part of the family. We all bring something—remember, I told you I'd take your cheesecakes for everyone to taste? So I was thinking, if your cheesecakes are going to be there, why shouldn't you be there, too?"

"Me?" Heddy said, not hiding her shock.

"Sure, you. You're the person responsible for our dessert. You should be there to eat dinner and dessert with us, and then to take a bow."

Did a grant recipient refuse an invitation to dinner with the grant-giver?

Heddy thought it was probably poor form.

But this didn't really seem to be a business invitation. This felt more personal. Like something private between herself and Lang.

Then Lang leaned forward again and confirmed her suspicions. "Besides, I'd like it if you came. I'd like it so much that I'll come out here and pick you up and bring you home."

That shouldn't have been the deciding factor.

And yet it was. Because more than feeling any sort of obligation or duty or debt, Heddy was weighing spending another long, long Sunday alone against spending it with this man she'd already decided she would have a second date with. If she were dating.

Which she wasn't.

"What time?" she asked, as if that might influence her decision.

"I'd be here about four-thirty. Dinner is fairly early—six—but we all start getting there around five, have a drink, some appetizers, meet anyone new…"

"Isn't this a little late to add a guest?"

"Never. There's always plenty to eat and drink, and GiGi believes the more the merrier. Plus, she wants to meet you. If not this week then I'd say you can count on her finagling a way to invite you herself next week. Besides," he said with a grin and a nod toward Carter, "you know I'm going to end up with your blanket again. This way I'll be able to return it."

"True."

"So will you come?"

Heddy thought about it. Weighed it. Knew her mother would hate it.

But it was only common courtesy to accept an invitation to meet the people funding her new business venture.

"Okay," she said, agreeing less than heartily, the same way she'd agreed to everything else Lang had presented her with.

Except that where before her tentative agreement had been tinged with doubt and worry, this time her feelings were edging far more toward something else. Something like a secret excited anticipation that she didn't want to have…

"Great!" Lang said, pushing away from the counter and reaching to squeeze her arm as if his enthusiasm just forced him to touch her.

The gesture took Heddy by surprise and was over even as it registered. She was left staring after him as he went around the island counter to get to the living room.

Her arm was still tingling with that simple contact and her traitorous mind was still regretting that she may have missed out on a kiss earlier, but Heddy used the time it took Lang to scoop up Carter—blanket and all—to regroup. To remind herself that there wasn't—and couldn't ever be—anything personal going on between them. Certainly not kissing.

Then she met them at her back door to open it for them.

"Dinner was fantastic. Thanks for cooking for us," he said with the sleeping child in his arms between them.

"I enjoyed it," Heddy confessed.

"See you tomorrow at four-thirty."

"Fancy dress or…?"

"Comfortable casual but not jeans. GiGi doesn't think jeans should be worn to Sunday dinner."

"Okay, got it," Heddy confirmed.

She expected Lang to go out, so she pushed open the screen door and held it for him. But he didn't move. Instead he stood there for another minute, with Carter acting as a safety bar between them, looking at Heddy in a way she couldn't decipher.

Then he smiled a small smile and leaned over enough to kiss her on the temple as if he just had to, despite her earlier dodge.

He followed up instantly with a "Good night," and finally went out the door.

Leaving Heddy to call, "Good night, drive safe," after him as if nothing had happened.

But something had happened.

She could still feel where his mouth had pressed against her skin for that split second.

And she liked it.

She felt guilty for liking it.

But she liked it nevertheless.

Which didn't seem possible because the kiss hadn't come from Daniel…

## *Chapter Five*

"Roardaroys."

"Yep, corduroys," Lang confirmed. "We have to dress up some for Sunday dinner at GiGi's."

"ZsiZsi for dinner. I wanna go."

"Good, because you are. That's why we just put on your nice shirt and your corduroys. Now I have to take a shower and change my clothes, then we'll pick up Heddy and come back this way to GiGi's. You want to watch some Curious George or some turtles while I get ready?"

"Ninzsa Tortles!" Carter decreed excitedly. Then he charged Lang's king-size bed, climbed up and hopped like a frog to the head of it where he got into position facing the entertainment center and lounged on the pillows like a sultan.

Lang started one of the DVDs he now kept in his bedroom to occupy the child while he showered, shaved and dressed every day.

With Carter's attention on the television, Lang closed and locked the bedroom door. He'd learned the hard way—with permanent marker on a downstairs wall—to contain Carter as much as possible when he couldn't keep his eye on him.

In the connecting bathroom, Lang stepped into the shower, calculating how long he had to get ready as he turned on the water.

He had to go all the way from his place in Cherry Creek, which was deep in the heart of Denver, out to suburban Arcada for Heddy, then back to Cherry Creek to GiGi's.

Deciding that he didn't have much time to waste, he did a fast shampoo and an equally fast lather-up before standing under the spray to rinse off.

He didn't mind the hurry or the back-and-forth drive he'd be doing, though, because it *was* for Heddy.

That thought sounded an alarm in his head.

It wasn't as if he'd sworn off women since Audrey—Carter was proof of that—it was just that Audrey had left him disinclined to go too far out on a limb with any woman again. Let alone too far out of his way—and Cherry Creek to Arcada, then back to Cherry Creek, then back to Arcada to take Heddy home, was definitely out of his way.

And yes, he was beginning to wonder if he wasn't going a little bit out on a limb with the woman, too.

Why the hell else had he wanted to kiss her so badly last night that even after she'd obviously rebuffed him the first time, he'd still caught her off guard and kissed her on the damn forehead later?

Not that it was a *damn* forehead. Like the rest of her, it was a beautiful forehead.

It was just that he didn't understand why, after she'd given the no signal, he'd still been so driven to kiss her that he had anyway, even if only on the temple.

And now this: a record-breaking quick shower and a whole lot of drive time. All for Heddy.

What was going on with him?

In the past three and a half years he'd been told by numerous women that he was guarded; that he was removed and remote; that he was emotionally unavailable. And he didn't deny any of it. So how was it that this particular woman was getting in under the radar?

This particular woman with whom he was not only doing business—and he didn't mix business with pleasure—but also this particular woman with whom the Camdens already had a bad track record.

Since Audrey, he made sure to keep things simple with women. Clean. Cut and dry. Under control.

After what he'd gone through with her—and getting over her—he was determined that nobody got in too far, and no marks were left getting out.

And if Audrey hadn't been lesson enough, which she had been, now, on top of it, there was Carter.

Not only had he become insta-dad, but Carter's existence had served as an eye-opener to how a casual fling could still get complicated.

Learning that there was even a chance that he could be a father had left him feeling the need to be more cautious than ever. He hadn't so much as gone to dinner with a woman since the possibility of parenthood had started. He hadn't so much as *wanted* to go near a woman since then.

Until Heddy Hanrahan.

Who was the absolute wrong woman for him to be getting involved with.

Even if he didn't have his nothing-but-a-little-hobby policy with women, even if he didn't have Carter to remind him how much deeper things could get than he thought they were getting, even if he wasn't dealing with being insta-dad and wasn't mixing business with pleasure, there was no way—*no* way—he could have a personal relationship with Heddy of all people. It would be adding insult to injury after what his father had done with her mother, and he could not, under any circumstances, let that disastrous history repeat itself.

Not that it could *completely* repeat itself, he thought as he dried off.

When his father's romantic relationship with her mother had died out, his father hadn't wanted to continue to see or to deal with Kitty Hanrahan in any way. He'd wanted to pretend she no longer existed.

That was the real reason behind Camden Incorporated cutting ties with Hanrahans Bakery and using a different supplier. The reason his father had persuaded his grandfather and brother not to help Harry Hanrahan expand to meet demand. And the reason that Hanrahans had ultimately gone under.

The grant and new business arrangement with Heddy were to make amends for all of that. So in that sense, there was no chance of history repeating itself, as far as the business end was concerned.

But the personal part?

As Lang went from the bathroom into the closet that also served as a dressing room, he thought about last night.

About wanting to kiss Heddy so much that he'd actually *stolen* a damn kiss. Like a kid.

He just hadn't been able to stop himself.

Stunning, sweet, funny, easy-to-be-with Heddy Hanrahan somehow seemed to be getting in under the radar.

And he didn't seem able to fight it.

It was just tough.

He liked her. He liked her in a way he hadn't liked anyone in a long, long while.

They clicked. And there was no explanation for that when it happened. It just did.

Now here he was—his pulse raced with every glimpse of her, he hated to say goodbye when he needed to leave her and he wanted to be with her again the minute he did.

Now here he was—thinking more about every detail of the way she looked, about the sound of her voice, about how to get her to smile or laugh, than about the business at hand.

Now here he was—thinking about her every minute he was away from her, incapable of closing his eyes without the image of her there in his mind.

But it just couldn't be, he told himself firmly as he combed his hair then roughly ran his hands through it to muss it up slightly.

He didn't *want* it to be.

He wanted to make up to the Hanrahan family for what his father had done. He wanted to see Heddy succeed. And yeah, he wanted to be the one who got her there.

But that was all he wanted.

No relationship. No romance. Nothing serious.

So no more kissing! Lips, temple, anywhere!

He slipped his feet into his handmade Italian loafers and returned to the bedroom where Carter didn't even glance at him.

But he addressed the child as if Carter were in on all the thoughts that had been going through his head. "I'll tell you what we're going to do, pal. We're going to get her business up and running as fast as we can, and then we're making tracks away from her. And in the meantime, it's business and nothing but business."

Carter took his eyes away from the television to look at him as if he were crazy.

"You being around should keep me on course, shouldn't it?" Lang asked the toddler.

"Immuh not round," Carter argued as if that was all he could glean from what Lang was saying.

Lang used the remote to turn off the DVD and television, then unlocked the bedroom door. "Get your shoes so we can put them on and go."

"Hetty an' ZsiZsi an' Zsorzse!" Carter confirmed, letting Lang know he intended to bring his stuffed monkey.

"Yeah, you can bring George," Lang confirmed, feeling indulgent and thinking that maybe it was good that his female family members had forced him to care for Carter.

If anything was a glaring reminder to keep him and a

situation with a woman under tight control, it was suddenly finding himself raising a kid.

And when it came to Heddy, he seemed to need a little extra reminder.

"Forget the last name. Forget the stores. Forget the grant. Forget everything! I'm taking you to my grandmother's house for Sunday dinner and that's all there is to this."

"Uh-huh…" Heddy responded dubiously to Lang's reassurance.

She'd been too nervous about this dinner to even glance at the grant paperwork and business contract that Lang had brought. Now she'd spent the drive from her place to Cherry Creek asking questions about protocol. Was his grandmother called Mrs. Camden or did she have a different last name? Would the dinner be sit-down or buffet? Should she cut and serve the cheesecakes, or would some sort of kitchen staff be doing that? Did all of his family know who she was and about the previous connection with Hanrahans Bakery? Did they all know about the grant and that she was basically an employee? Did they appreciate having their Sunday family dinner invaded by someone who was going to work for them?

And on and on the questions had come until Lang had laughingly told her to relax.

"You're not going to Buckingham Palace, you know. And we aren't nose-in-the-air kind of people. Is that how you see me?"

It wasn't. Not at all.

But Heddy didn't answer him because right as he said that, he turned off Gaylord Street onto a stone-paved lane that led up to a house that made her eyes widen in awe.

The house was a two-story, brick-and-stucco Tudor mansion that curved in a semicircle away from a five-car garage. The steep roof was dotted with dormers and two brick chimneys. There were shutters framing all the windows and ivy growing up the walls to just under the gables.

The centerpiece of the meticulously manicured grounds was an elaborate fountain surrounded by the circular drive. A redbrick wall kept the entire property enclosed, and while there weren't turrets or a moat, Heddy thought the house that towered above it all was very castlelike. And intimidating.

"It's a little like a palace," Heddy muttered in awe.

"Nah, it's just a big old house. A *nice* big old house, but still, just a big old house."

It was the kind of place that Heddy drove by and wondered what it must be like on the inside.

And who could possibly afford to live in it.

She'd worn one of her best pairs of gray wool slacks and a white cowl-necked sweater that Clair had given her for Christmas—what she considered dressy casual as spelled out by Lang the night before. But looking at the Camden mansion made her wonder if she was still going to be underdressed.

She imagined that, in a place like this, everyone else's *dressy casual* would be designer labels—far better than what she had on. And she suddenly felt like Cinderella going to the ball *without* the benefit of a fairy godmother's help.

"I don't know about this," she said.

Lang had parked behind the line of luxury vehicles that hugged the curb of the drive and turned off the engine. He didn't ignore her alarm but instead reached over and covered her hand with his, squeezing tight.

"It'll be fine, you'll see," he said comfortingly. "Think of this place as a frat house or a dormitory—barely big enough to handle the ten kids who ended up here. It's just home."

Hardly the three-bedroom, ranch-style, cookie-cutter track house she'd grown up in and had called home.

But having Lang's hand covering hers was sending a glittery sensation through her that served as a distraction and actually did help. Despite the fact that it also set off a bit of a red flag because she liked having him touch her more than she wanted to like it.

That was something to worry about later, though.

"'Just home,'" she repeated as if that might convince her.

"Come on, you'll see," Lang assured her, tightening his grip once more before he released her hand and got out of the SUV.

Lang unstrapped Carter from his car seat and lifted the toddler to the ground. Heddy got out, too, regretting that she'd let him persuade her to do this.

"ZsiZsi!" Carter said excitedly, running for the oak front door with leaded glass in its upper half that rose high above a wide, curved three-step landing. Obviously he was familiar enough with the place to also feel at home here.

But rather than follow the boy, Heddy met Lang at the rear of the SUV to help him unload the cheesecakes and carry them in.

The cheesecakes were in separate boxes, which Lang had stacked in two larger boxes to aid transport. He handed the lighter of the two to Heddy and took the one with more cheesecakes in it for himself. Slinging it onto his left hip, he closed the rear hatch.

Then he turned to Heddy, whose continuing discomfort must have shown in her face because one glance at her made him grin and shake his head at her.

"I'm really not taking you to stand in front of a firing squad. Honest, it will be fine—nobody bites," he said, putting his free arm around her shoulders to urge her toward the house.

Having his arm around her was yet another distraction. A big one because Heddy was suddenly hyperaware of being tucked into Lang's side, enveloped by that long, muscular arm.

But it was nothing more than a friendly gesture, she told herself. To bolster her confidence. It wasn't a hot, hunky man who looked terrific in brown tweed slacks and a cream-colored cashmere mock turtleneck sweater putting his arm around her in some romantic way. It was just someone who knew she was nervous offering her reassurance.

Yet when they reached the front door and he let go of her to open it, she wilted a little in disappointment.

"ZsiZsi?" Carter called as he charged into the enormous foyer with its high vaulted ceiling and crystal chandelier that hung over a large round entry table.

To the right was what appeared to be a formal living room where people were mingling. An elderly woman was standing in the connecting archway. At the sound of Carter's voice, she turned, bent and opened her arms, calling out an affectionate, "There's my boy!"

Carter wasted no time running into those open arms and hugging her effusively around the neck while announcing, "I brought Zsorzse."

"Then we'll get out the monkey food," the elderly woman said before she sent Carter into the throng of people and came into the foyer with a welcoming smile on her lined face.

"Hi, GiGi," Lang greeted, kissing her on the cheek when she got near enough.

"Hello to one of my other favorite boys," she said, winking at Heddy as she hugged Lang.

"And you must be Heddy," the older woman stated when she'd released her grandson.

"Heddy Hanrahan, this is my grandmother—"

"I'm GiGi. Everyone calls me that and I barely answer to anything else anymore."

"Nice to meet you," Heddy said softly, taking in the sight of the woman Kitty Hanrahan had once expected to have as a mother-in-law.

Georgianna Camden was not more than five feet tall and had a grandmotherly shape—not fat but fluffy. She was wearing a mauve pantsuit that was classic but not stuffy. Her salt-and-pepper hair was short and curly around a face that still showed signs of glowing beauty.

Heddy wasn't sure whether it was the Mrs. Claus pink cheeks or the sparkle in her blue eyes, but she exuded an earthy warmth and friendliness that went a long way in making Heddy begin to relax.

Of course it didn't hurt that Lang was still very close beside her.

"We need to get these cheesecakes into the fridge, GiGi," Lang announced, adjusting his hold on the box.

"Oh, we're all looking forward to those! Margaret and I made space for them. Get them in the fridge before they're ruined," the older woman instructed just as the door opened and in came a man who resembled Lang, accompanied by a woman and an elderly gentleman, who went straight to GiGi and kissed her hello.

Lang made the introductions. "Cade, Nati, this is Heddy. Heddy, Cade is my cousin. Nati will be his better half when they set the date and get married. And that's Jonah Morrison—Nati's grandfather and GiGi's friend."

Quick greetings were exchanged before Lang led the way through the entry, past a wide, curving staircase with carved oak posts and banister. They ended up in a homey restaurant-size kitchen with a tile floor, tarnished brass lighting and plumbing fixtures, and pristine white cupboards.

"Wow, dream kitchen." Heddy envied the space, which contained a commercial-size refrigerator/freezer, a six-burner gas stove with a built-in grill, double ovens, a triad of sinks, an expansive island in the center of the room for workspace and a breakfast nook large enough to hold a conference table.

"We spent a lot of time here fixing those dinners that gave me the mad chopping skills you saw at work last night," he said as he opened the refrigerator and began to load cheesecake boxes into it.

When they were finished, Lang showed her a second way out of the kitchen, leading them through a dining room set up for a buffet service and into the formal living room from a different direction.

More introductions were made—too many for Heddy to keep track of even though she tried. The one constant with every Camden she met, though, was that same down-to-earth warmth and friendliness that she'd found in both Lang and his grandmother. The Camdens had a true gift, Heddy decided, for casting off whatever status their name might carry. Lang had been right—there were no noses in the air, nothing intimidating about any of them. By the time Lang's cousin Jani raised her voice to say she had an announcement, Heddy was beginning to actually feel at home.

"So, I know you've all seen me go through years of silly, unnecessary worrying about my sad single ovary," Jani said when she had silence and every eye was upon her. The attractive man who'd been introduced as Gideon Thatcher was now standing beside her.

"In keeping with the theme of moving fast..." Jani said with an adoring glance at the man who was holding her hand and beaming back at her. "Not only did we meet, fall in love and get married within five weeks, but here we are, on almost our second month anniversary with another announcement. We know people say not to tell this early, but I just can't wait. We heard from the doctor on Friday and..." She paused as if there was a drumroll, then nearly shouted, "There's a baby on board!"

As cheers and congratulations were shouted and family members rushed the obviously happy couple, Lang leaned close to Heddy's ear and explained, "Jani wasn't sure she was *ever* going to be able to have kids and there was nothing she wanted more, so this is sort of a mini-miracle."

The news put a lump in Heddy's throat but she plastered a smile on her face and nodded.

Then she took a big drink of the wine Lang had brought her and prayed for strength to get through the rest of the evening now focused on celebrating the happy couple's baby news.

An evening not too unlike one she herself had had with Daniel.

Once upon a time.

"Lie and tell me it wasn't too bad," Lang said when they were finally back in his SUV.

Carter was in the car seat behind them, softly singing along to something he was watching on Lang's smartphone. It was just past eight o'clock and they were driving away from Georgianna Camden's house, headed for Arcada.

"I don't have to lie," Heddy answered. "It wasn't bad at all. I've never been anywhere with so many strangers who all had the knack for making me feel like we were old friends."

Lang cast her a smile. "Maybe you even enjoyed it a little," he said hopefully.

"I did," she admitted, without telling him about the darker feelings that had been stirred over the baby announcement.

Because truthfully, while she'd expected those darker feelings to drag her down for the rest of the evening, that wasn't what had happened. And it was all due to Lang. He had stayed by her side or included her in whatever he needed to do with Carter so she hadn't ever been left to fend for herself. He had kept the tone light, he'd joked with her, teased her, made it easy to recall names when members of his family came to chat and injected funny stories about his cousins and siblings to make her laugh.

He had been so attentive and charming and fun that he'd actually accomplished what nothing and no one in the past five years had accomplished—he'd made her escape the darker feelings altogether not long after they'd appeared. He'd made her forget everything but him, and she actually *had* ended up having a good time.

"So you're the baby of that family, huh?"

Even in the dim car interior lit only by streetlights she saw him grimace. "You'll never know how much I hated it when one of my older brothers or cousins called me a baby," he grumbled. "Yes, Lindie, Livi and I—and Jani who is the same age—are the youngest."

"And you didn't like that?" Heddy asked.

"There were six boys in the same house who were all older than I was. Three *girls* who were my age. What do you think?"

Heddy shrugged. "My brother and I pretty much went our separate ways, so I don't know."

"It was bad until I could hold my own with the older boys. They didn't want anything to do with me because I was *the baby.* That was what they'd say when I wanted in on whatever they were doing. 'Go play with the girls, you're a baby.' That left me with only three girls to play with and that was a clique I didn't fit into."

"Even as a triplet? I thought twins and triplets had some sort of special bond."

"The bond was among the three girls. I was odd-man-out with the whole lot."

"That doesn't sound good. Were you a sad little outcast as a kid?" Heddy asked with a sympathetic laugh.

It bought her another glance from him, this one accompanied by a smile that she realized at that moment had the power to send tiny shards of delight all through her. But she tried to ignore it.

"At first we were all sad kids."

"Oh, sure," Heddy said in a hurry, regrouping when she remembered how they'd all come to live at GiGi's house. "The plane crash. You lost your parents and your grandfather, and you had to move."

"So yeah, at first there was a lot of sadness and grief and upheaval."

"*And* you didn't have anyone to play with even in a house with nine other kids."

"Pretty much," he confirmed, laughing again.

"At least you had each other," Heddy said, looking for a silver lining somewhere.

"I'd say that we had GiGi. And H.J. and Margaret and Louie. It took a little more time for all ten of us to 'have each other.' We did get there, though. We're stuck together like glue now. We're there for each other through thick and thin, we run Camden Inc. together."

"So how long did it take for the other boys to stop seeing you as *the baby?*"

"It varied. I basically fought my way up the ladder or outsmarted them or did something to prove I *wasn't* a baby."

"You literally fought with some of them?"

"We were boys. Rough-and-tumble boys."

"So it was a jungle inside that beautiful house."

"With ten kids and seven of them boys? A little bit."

Heddy could just imagine Lang in nothing but a loincloth.

Naked chest. Broad shoulders. She guessed that he had great pecs. And no doubt hard, washboard abs and thickly muscled thighs…

She shook off the fantasy to say, "And before you started working your way up the food chain? What did you do, just play alone?"

He laughed at that, too. "A little. But I also hung out a lot with Louie, which is probably how I came to be the start-up guy with Camden Inc. He was like a father figure to me. I think early on he felt bad seeing me left out of everything with the other kids. He enlisted me as his *helper* and I'd followed him around, work in the yard with him, play assistant on his handyman jobs. I learned a lot from Louie. He's a very methodical person and he taught me about starting projects from the ground up."

"Just like a father."

"Yeah. He was also who I called when I had my first fender bender, and when a girl's father caught me up a tree."

"Up a tree?" Heddy asked with a curious laugh.

"Her bedroom was on the second floor. There was a big tree just outside it. We had a—" Lang shot Heddy another glance and smiled wickedly "—*rendezvous* planned. I was supposed to climb up the tree, slither across the branch that would get me to her room and…"

"Her father caught you," Heddy finished for him. "Did Louie save you?"

"He did. He couldn't save me from owning up to the fender-bender because I got a ticket and the police and the insurance company got involved. But he was a good buffer between me and an angry GiGi."

"But when you were up the tree?"

"Louie came to the girl's house, reasoned with the father, assured him it would never happen again."

"And didn't tell your grandmother?"

"It was our secret. But that doesn't mean I got away with anything. Louie gave me the talks—the embarrassing birds-and-bees talk, the respect-women talk—"

"Apparently not the condom talk," Heddy teased with a nod at Carter in the backseat.

"Oh, no, I got the no-sex-but-here's-a-condom-just-in-case talk and the condom to go along with it. I even got the sometimes-things-fail talk. I just didn't believe it until there was proof."

They'd reached her house by then, and Heddy was sorry to have the time she'd spent with Lang end. Listening to the tales of his childhood had made the drive home go by too quickly and she would have liked the evening to continue.

But Carter was asleep with his head against the back of the car seat, so she knew the night was over.

However, as she opened the door and got out—thinking to just say thanks and good-night—Lang cracked the windows, left the heat on, put the emergency brake on and got out of the SUV, too.

"I can go up alone, you shouldn't leave—"

"He'll be okay," Lang said, glancing at Carter, who didn't wake when they closed their doors.

Lang *had* parked within a few feet of her back door. Had Carter so much as snored they would have been able to hear it.

As Heddy searched through her purse for her keys, Lang said, "So your cheesecakes were a big hit. I don't think my family could have loved them more."

Heddy laughed. "I might have thought they were just being nice except that there were so many complaints about not having any left to take home."

"They weren't just being nice," he assured her while she continued to rummage through her purse. "Tomorrow is the inspection of your new kitchen space—remember?"

"Oh, that's right," Heddy muttered with her face nearly inside her hobo bag.

"We should be there to make sure everything is on the up-and-up. I think everybody is honest, but a little supervision never hurts."

"Okay," Heddy said as she began to worry that she had somehow not taken her keys with her.

"The inspection is scheduled for one o'clock. How about I pick you up at twelve-thirty and we go over together?"

"I could meet you," Heddy offered.

"I'll be driving right by here, no sense taking two cars."

"Okay." It struck her then that she'd changed purses for tonight. And probably had left her keys in her other one.

With a sigh of self-disgust, she said, "I don't have my key to get in. I have one up there, hidden behind that rain gauge, but I have to get the ladder or a patio chair to stand on to reach it and I don't want to keep you from Carter for too long, so go ahead and—"

"Let's see if I can reach it."

"It's really high so I can see it out of my kitchen window," Heddy explained as she followed him off the landing to the spot beneath the rain gauge, standing behind him.

Lang *was* tall but not quite tall enough to reach it on his first attempt.

"I'm so close," he said. Looking at the ground beneath him, he found a large stone and positioned it so he could stand on it to try again.

With just that much of a boost he made it, and Heddy explained how to open the gauge to get the key out. But while he fiddled with it, the boulder fell from under him, pitching him sharply forward.

It was pure reflex that made Heddy grab him as he fell against the house.

"Are you all right?" she asked in alarm.

"You know, just a broken nose, it'll be fine," he said facetiously, laughing. "But thanks for the catch."

Her hands were still on him. On a *man's* hips for the first time in five years. On *Lang Camden's* hips…

"Sorry," she muttered, letting go of him.

"For what? Trying to catch me?"

"You know, for causing problems," she answered. She couldn't say she was apologizing for laying hands on him even though that *was* what she was fretting over. She'd had no business imagining him in a loincloth earlier but at least that had only been in her mind. This had been actual physical contact.

She stepped back enough for him to turn, not realizing that she'd left very little room for that until she found herself separated from him by mere inches.

But fearing that he actually might have hurt his face,

she gazed up into it with a nurse's eye rather than moving farther away.

Only it was really just the woman in her that registered that his ruggedly handsome features were none the worse for wear, and studying them so closely made something inside her go a little weak.

"You're not bleeding," she said, her own voice quiet from the effects of looking at him that way and being so near to him.

"I was teasing about the broken nose. I really am fine," he assured her, his tone deeper. "I've taken worse face slams than that, believe me."

He did have a smudge or a mark on his brow, though, and Heddy reached up to it. "There *is* something..."

She gently rubbed the shadow with her fingertips. His skin was smooth but not soft. Masculine...

"It's dirt, not a bruise," she concluded when part of the mark came off.

He didn't veer away from her attention; in fact he seemed to focus more intently on her in a moment that suddenly felt a little charged.

Then he took her completely off guard and kissed her.

Not on the temple, like the night before, but on the mouth. His lips pressed to hers so unexpectedly that for a moment Heddy's eyes opened wider, looking beyond him at the wall of her house. *Stop it!* That's what she thought she should say. She should push away from him and shout *Stop it!*

But then somehow she got swept away in that kiss.

Somehow her eyes closed and she actually thought she was kissing him back.

This man who wasn't Daniel.

The realization caused her to brace for a negative reaction. For the overwhelming sense that she was doing something horribly wrong.

But it didn't come despite the fact that she was very much aware that this wasn't Daniel. That this was Lang.

All Lang.

He kissed differently than Daniel. His mouth against hers felt different. But none of that was bad. In fact, it was good. This kiss was very, very good,

And not only were his lips moving over hers, hers were moving right with them, even parting just the slightest bit the same way his were.

*But this isn't Daniel...*

And yet as strange as it seemed, she didn't feel guilty. She didn't feel as if she was doing something she shouldn't be doing. Instead, she just liked it. It was nice....

Then it was over. Lang straightened, still gazing down at her, but with an expression that said his actions had taken him somewhat by surprise, too.

"Concussion?" he suggested.

"Maybe," Heddy concurred without any excuse for herself.

"Except that I feel fine," he nearly whispered with a smile that said he didn't want to make excuses. "Really, really fine."

So did she, which stunned her even more than the kiss. She felt really, really fine.

"And I got the key," Lang added, holding it up for her to take.

It only occurred to Heddy at that moment, when his glance dropped to her mouth and she thought he was going to kiss her again, that she was still standing very close to him.

And while she was inclined to stay right there and have him kiss her again, she wasn't sure if that might be tempting fate so she took a step back.

"I'm sorry," she apologized again. "It was stupid to leave my keys and if I hadn't—"

He shook his handsome head to stop the apology and took her hand to press the key into it "It was worth it."

She made a fist around the key and pulled her hand away from his, heading for her door again where she was quick to open it.

Then Lang was there with her, reaching in around her to turn on her kitchen light.

Turning her on a little, too, when that big body brushed against her ever so slightly and the heat of him wrapped her in warmth.

It was something purely instinctive that caused her to turn her face to look at him over her shoulder, to tilt her chin even though she was at an odd angle.

And odd angle or not, he kissed her a second time. A second long time. And she kissed him again, too, wondering if she'd gone a little crazy, before the kiss ended and he stepped back.

"I'll see you tomorrow," he said softly, sounding confused himself, though Heddy didn't understand why.

Then she went inside and closed the door, only listening for him to drive away as what had just happened began to sink in.

## *Chapter Six*

Heddy could tell that something wasn't quite right with Lang when he picked her up for the inspection of her new commercial kitchen space on Monday. To begin with, he was very late getting there. And while she'd always dealt directly with him, this time his secretary had called to tell her that Lang was running behind schedule.

To avoid further delays, Heddy watched for him so she could go out as soon as he arrived. As he pulled into her drive he was saying something over his shoulder to Carter that was obviously stern and it was clear he was not in a great mood.

When Lang greeted Heddy with an apology for keeping her waiting, his agitation didn't seem aimed at her. But she still couldn't help thinking that it might be a reaction to their kiss the night before. That he regretted it. That maybe he blamed her for it.

She hadn't been able to think about much except him

and those kisses since they'd happened. But in all of the confused emotions that had swept through her in the process, there hadn't been anything that had made her as out of sorts as he seemed to be. It was unnerving to think that might be his reaction.

He was a little hard on the inspector when they finally got to the new space, and he gave no quarter with the Realtors who were also there.

Watching him closely during the course of the inspection, Heddy began to see a pattern. Lang was all-business with the business people; he was more somber but still companionable with her. But he was having the most difficulty containing his temper when he dealt with Carter.

Carter, who *was* particularly wild and ornery throughout the inspection, and seemed no more pleased with Lang than Lang was with him. In fact, at one point when Lang took him to task, Carter's usually hard-to-understand vocabulary became perfectly clear when he shouted, "Grouch!"

It was when he pulled off his shoes for the third time, brought them to Lang and said, "Here, take eeze," and Heddy saw Lang's jaw clench, that Heddy decided it might be better if she left Lang to the inspection and took Carter aside to put his shoes back on herself.

"Maybe both of you guys got up on the wrong side of the bed this morning," she muttered as she did.

Apparently Carter thought he was supposed to respond to her comment, because he said, "I pooss uh phun in uh toy-et."

Heddy didn't quite follow that. "You put fun in the

toilet?" she asked, thinking he was talking about potty training in some fashion.

"No, uh *cephun,*" Carter corrected.

"You put Lang's cell phone in the toilet?" she asked.

"An my Mick-eye Mouse wash."

Heddy had noticed that Carter was only wearing one of his wristwatches today. "You put your Mickey Mouse watch and Lang's phone in the toilet," she translated.

"An a bad shoe. I fooshed 'em!" he confirmed.

"You flushed them?"

"Wa-er aw ober!"

"Water all over…" Heddy was getting the picture.

Just as she finished putting on his shoes, he gave her another indication of how Lang's morning had gone by taking them off again and repeating, "Take eeze. No shoes!"

"Oh, Carter." Heddy sighed, laughing quietly and knowing she shouldn't be as relieved as she was that the potential reason for Lang's sour mood didn't involve her or their kisses last night.

"You have to wear shoes, kiddo," she told Carter, putting them on again.

When the inspection ended, Lang told her everything looked good. There were a few minor things that the current owner had agreed to fix, but otherwise he thought they could set a closing date.

"Unless you've changed your mind," he added, letting her know it was up to her.

"No, I like the space more now than I did when we saw it before," she assured him. "And since Clair's husband and two other lawyers at his firm looked over the grant paperwork and the contract with Camden Superstores this morning and have given me a thumbs-up, I guess we're good to go all the way around."

"Great. Glad to hear it," Lang said.

Everything turned to business then while Lang picked Carter up and propped him on his hip to keep him out of any more mischief. When they were done, Heddy, Lang and Carter went out to the SUV.

"Are you busy the rest of today?" Lang asked as he put a wiggling, once-again-shoeless Carter into his car seat.

Thinking that Lang had something else business-related in mind—and wanting to prolong this time with him even if he wasn't in the best mood—she said, "My major plan was to figure out if April is too early to sprinkle grass seed on the spot where your crew took out my sign this morning. By the way, thank you for that. It was a bigger job than I thought and I couldn't have done it myself."

The men he'd sent over had also hung a big banner from the eaves of her house announcing that her cheesecakes would soon be available at Camden Superstores.

"Could I persuade you to do me a favor then?" he asked.

"Can I hear what the favor is before I say?" Where had that flirtatious tone come from?

He told her about his morning, confirming what she'd guessed from Carter's comments. During Lang's shower, Carter had apparently lost interest in what he was supposed to have been watching on television and had instead tried to flush unflushable objects, causing the toilet to back up and flood the bathroom. Not to mention putting Lang's smartphone out of commission.

"I have my phone buried in a bowl of rice. One of my sisters said that might dry it out and bring it back," Lang said. "But I run my whole life on that thing, so I can't take the chance that it will come back with kinks. I'm just gonna get a new phone, so I need to go down to the mall in Cherry Creek and I don't think I can do that alone with Carter today."

Heddy still had moments when something about the boy made her think of Tina and stabbed her through the heart, but for the most part being with Carter wasn't painful for her now. Somewhere along the way she'd come to view Carter merely as Carter and had stopped dreading being with the toddler. In fact, sometimes she got a kick out of him and his energy and boundless enthusiasm for things.

Since she could tell that Lang really needed some help today, she said, "As of today my shop is closed so I think I could probably fit a trip to the mall into my busy schedule. And while we're there, you might want to have Carter's feet measured. His shoes are kind of hard to get on, maybe they're too small and that's why he keeps taking them off."

Light dawned in Lang's strikingly handsome face. "Oh, that makes sense! A shoe from a different pair was in the mass flushing today and he said it was a bad shoe. I just figured he was screwing around. I didn't think it really meant anything."

Heddy smiled, glad to see that his dark spirits were evaporating right in front of her eyes. "I think he's just outgrown them and they hurt his feet."

"Sure. And that makes them bad. Of course. Well,

like I said, I'm a rookie. And maybe a little dense, too, huh?"

"I don't think that at all. I think raising a child is a learn-as-you-go kind of thing in a lot of ways. And you're doing pretty well for being new at it," she said as they got into the front seats of the SUV and headed for Denver.

It was Heddy's mood that darkened as the time at Cherry Creek Mall passed.

After they'd successfully purchased a new smartphone and three pairs of shoes for Carter—who *did* need them—Carter spotted the children's play area at one end of the lower level. It had bigger-than-life cartoon characters for kids to crawl under, climb on and slide and jump off.

Of course Carter was drawn there and Heddy didn't have the heart to say no when Lang was willing to indulge the toddler, so she conceded. Feeling, even as she did, that she was approaching her own private hell. She might have gotten better about being with Carter, but watching an entire group of kids of varying ages, some of them little girls, was still like opening a wound.

Trying to hide that fact, she sat with Lang at one of the café tables outside the half wall that surrounded the play area. Using his new phone, Lang checked in with his office, leaving Heddy with nothing to do but watch all the kids at play. And while she tried hard to focus only on Carter, her attention still wandered to the other kids. Particularly to a little girl who looked to be about the age Tina would have been now—another trigger for pain.

But then it got worse.

After sending an older child into the play area, a woman pushed a stroller right next to Heddy's chair and stopped. Heddy couldn't keep herself from looking down at the baby girl inside the stroller. A baby girl who had to be no older than Tina had been.

Three months.

And to make matters worse, the baby had just a smattering of thin, pale, wispy hair like Tina had had.

And big brown eyes like Tina's.

And chubby, cherubic cheeks and a tiny petal-pink mouth.

Just like Tina…

And that did Heddy in. It took everything she had not to cry. Not to get up and run as fast as she could from that spot and that baby.

*Keep it together,* she silently screamed at herself.

But to do that she turned herself to stone on the outside. Sitting straighter and much, much stiffer, she stared at the passersby rather than at the kids in the play area or at the baby in the stroller, and fought just to maintain the appearance that she wasn't falling apart inside.

"Okay, done!" Lang finally said.

Heddy stiffly turned her head to Lang and hoped that the sadness that was nearly overwhelming her didn't show on her face.

"As if this day couldn't get any crazier," Lang said to himself. Then, to Heddy he said, "We're all really conscious of not abusing the privilege, but at Camden Inc. a request from a Camden is granted ASAP. We have the manpower to accomplish just about anything. Then take into account that the request is top priority and I want it fast-tracked—because I know you can't afford slow movement on any of this—and as a result…"

He shrugged as if he were finally conceding to the way this day was playing out.

"My secretary tells me that there's a bakery near here that's going out of business. She just heard through a friend that the almost-new ovens, refrigerators and freezers are all going up for sale and she can get us first look if we go over there now. And if that's not enough, because I put a rush on them, the mock-ups of your packaging, logos and the initial promo ads that our marketing and advertising departments have been working on for you came in this afternoon. So if you don't mind, after we drag Carter out of there, we can run over to look at the appliances, and then—if you want—we can go to my office and check out the other stuff. You can either green-light the designs or send them back to the drawing board."

Distractions. That was good, Heddy told herself.

And yet somehow it wasn't helping to pull her out of the pit she'd slipped into.

"What do you say?" Lang asked when she didn't immediately answer.

"Sure," she agreed quietly, thinking that filling what remained of the day with activity was better than going home and being alone when she felt like this.

"Where did he go?"

There was an edge of panic in Lang's voice when he suddenly realized that Carter was not where he was supposed to be.

After looking at and buying some of the industrial-size appliances that Heddy would need, and then going to Lang's office to check the packaging and promotional material, it was after seven before they'd headed back to Heddy's house with a bag of burgers and fries. When they were done with the meal, Carter had demanded the "plillow and banket" that Heddy had given him before and gone to lie on her sofa to watch cartoons while Lang and she stayed at the kitchen table and chatted.

Lang had just glanced over at the couch and discovered that Carter wasn't there.

"Carter?" he called as he got up from the table.

Heddy's back had been to the sofa so she hadn't seen Carter move. She stood and went with Lang to search for the two-and-a-half-year-old who wasn't answering.

"At least I don't hear a toilet flushing," Lang grumbled. But they didn't find Carter anywhere in the living room, kitchen or shop area out front. Or in the downstairs bathroom, either.

"I don't know how he could have gone up the stairs without either of us noticing," Heddy said. "But he couldn't have gotten outside because the doors are all closed tight, and the door down to my work space creaks like crazy. If he'd opened it, we would have heard it. So let's look upstairs," she suggested, leading the way to the bedrooms and bath there. "He has to be somewhere. Does he like to hide?"

"Yeah, but he's not good at it. He thinks he's hidden if he stands against a wall with his eyes closed," Lang said as they climbed the steps that were enclosed on both sides and rose from just behind the kitchen wall of Heddy's stove and pantry.

They found Carter in the larger of the two bedrooms

on the second floor. He'd climbed onto Heddy's queen-size bed and was sound asleep, clutching the toy he called Baby tightly against his tiny chest.

"The couch must not have been enough for him tonight," Lang whispered.

"He had a long, hard day," Heddy said just as softly.

"I'll carry him back down—"

Heddy reflexively stopped Lang with a hand to his arm, immediately aware of just how rock-solid an arm it was but trying not to let that register as something she liked. A lot.

"It's okay," she said. "Let him stay where he is while we have dessert. No sense moving him now and then again when you take him home. He's fine there."

"You don't mind?"

Heddy shook her head and crossed to the bed to pull a corner of her quilt over the little boy to cover him.

Then she and Lang quietly went back down the stairs.

The oven timer began dinging as they reached the kitchen and Heddy opened the oven door to check the sugar cookies she was baking for their dessert. The oversize cookies needed another minute or more, and after telling Lang that, the two of them gathered what was left of their fast-food meal and threw it away.

By the time that was done, the cookies were ready to come out and since tonight her sofa was free, Heddy suggested they sit there and have dessert.

When they were settled, Lang said, "How come being with you improved *my* day and put me in a much, much better mood, but being with me has made you more quiet than usual and..." He studied her with those gorgeous blue eyes. "Sad?" She knew she *had* been quieter than usual but she thought she'd hidden her plummeting spirits better than that.

"I'm sorry," she said. "It isn't…anything."

"I think it is," he insisted. "I've been feeling it for a while. Since the mall. Something's wrong. If I did something or said something…"

"You didn't." She couldn't let him take the blame for inadvertently placing her on the sidelines of that play area.

"Don't you feel well? Did I give you a headache? Are you tired of having Carter around? Or me? Or—"

Heddy laughed but even that came out sounding gloomy. "I feel fine." Physically, anyway. "It's just… me…"

He didn't look convinced by the "it's not you, it's me" line. Instead his expression was growing more concerned by the minute. And that didn't seem fair so Heddy decided she should just tell him. There wasn't any reason not to, anyway. She hadn't wanted to get into this part of her history with him before, but something was different now. Maybe that he'd shared some of his own personal stuff with her.

"I have a hard time being around kids," she confessed.

"So it *is* Carter."

She laughed again, this time with more humor. "Carter is great," she said, meaning it. "He's such a character and he's so busy and so full of life—" And just saying that last word made her voice crack.

"But he's a handful and he can run you ragged," Lang concluded as if to let her know he understood if she'd grown weary of the child.

"No, really, it isn't Carter. In fact, being with Carter has actually been good for me. This is the first time in five years that I've been able to handle being around a kid at all, let alone as much as I've been around him."

"Why?" Lang asked, sounding completely confused as he reached for another cookie from the plate Heddy had set on the coffee table. "I know you said at one point that you'd been married. Was having kids the issue that broke it up?"

"The marriage didn't break up. And not only was I married, I had a little girl. She was three months old when I lost them both."

That stopped Lang cold. "Lost? As in—"

"They died." She watched shock hit him.

"Oh, God, Heddy, I'm so sorry. It didn't even occur to me—"

"I know. If I say I *was* married, people automatically assume I'm divorced. That's just more common than becoming a widow at twenty-five."

"Was there a car accident?" he asked before quickly adding, "You don't have to talk about it if you don't want to."

"*Not* talking about it doesn't fix it. And no, it wasn't a car accident. It was a freak thing. I'd been on maternity leave..."

"From your job as a nurse?"

"A pediatric nurse, right," she confirmed. "Tina—that was my baby's name—was three months old and I had to go back to work. My husband, Daniel, and I didn't want to leave the baby in day care or with a sitter if at all possible, so I asked for the overnight shifts at the hospital. That way Daniel could be with Tina while I worked, and when I got home, he went to work."

"What did he do?"

"He was a teacher. High school physics."

Lang had stopped eating the cookies and was listening very intently, his gaze steady on her as she continued.

"My first night back at the hospital was also the first really cold night of that autumn. We had an appointment set up for a guy to come out and check the furnace—it was something we did most years—but that wasn't for a few days. It hadn't ever been a big deal to turn the heat on *before* the furnace had been checked, and with the baby..." Heddy's voice cracked but she was determined not to cry so she swallowed and went on. "Not thinking anything of it, we decided to turn on the heat. No big deal."

"Except that it was?"

"There was a carbon monoxide leak. We didn't have detectors, there wasn't any kind of warning. Daniel and Tina went to sleep that night and...I lost them both."

Lang's handsome face showed even more shock—his eyes were wide, his brows arched high. "That *is* a freak thing," he agreed.

For a moment he didn't say anything else; he just reached over and took her hand. Then, in a deeper, slightly hushed voice, he said, "Did it happen here? Did you come home and find them?"

"It wasn't here, no. It was in another house. I sold it. I couldn't go back there."

"Yeah, I don't think I'd be able to, either."

"And no, I didn't find them. I'm grateful for that at

least. Daniel had an early meeting that morning so Clair was coming over to stay with Tina until I got home. But when Clair got there Daniel didn't answer the door. So she went looking in the windows..."

Even though Heddy hadn't seen with her own eyes what her cousin had seen, there was still a vivid enough image of it in her mind. "When Clair got to our bedroom window without seeing Daniel or Tina anywhere in the house, she knocked on the glass, thinking maybe Daniel had overslept. You know, maybe he'd been up late with Tina and then they'd both conked out..."

"Sure."

"But when there was no answer to the knock on the window, either, she peeked through a tiny gap in the bedroom curtains. She could see Daniel, under the covers..."

And in her mind's eye, so could Heddy. With the bassinet at the foot of the bed.

"But even though Clair knocked harder on the window and started calling really loudly to Daniel..." Another catch in Heddy's throat kept her from saying what Lang finished for her.

"Daniel didn't wake up."

Heddy shook her head and fought for the ability to talk around the lump in her throat, still staving off tears. "It didn't make Tina cry, either. Not even when Clair hit the window hard enough to crack it and shouted at the top of her lungs. Clair realized then that something was wrong. She called Clark, who was her fiancé at the time, and he called 9-1-1 and rushed over. By the time I got home there were police and fire trucks and an ambulance...."

Lang looked as if he were picturing it all himself and wished he wasn't. "That's horrible," he commiserated, and then, as if the light dawned for him, he added, "and today there was that little baby in the stroller, right next to you. I saw you looking at her. I thought you went a little pale, but—" He made a pained face. "I thought maybe she had a dirty diaper and smelled bad or something."

Heddy managed a faint smile at that. "No, she just reminded me of Tina. And that I don't have her anymore. Being around a lot of kids—"

"Must always make you think of your own baby," Lang concluded. "And what did I do? I've been bringing Carter over here, I put you at the edge of a play area full of kids and made you a sitting duck for a mother with a stroller… I'm sorry! If I had known… Why didn't you just say no to the play area today?"

"After Carter had already seen Buz Bunny?" Heddy said with a small smile of appreciation for the little boy's pronunciation. "It's been five years," she said. "Seems silly that I couldn't do something that simple."

"Things in life that hit us hard change us," he said as if speaking from experience of his own. "What we can and can't do changes."

"Still, being around Carter *has* sort of reconditioned me, now that I'm thinking about it. I've stopped trying to imagine Tina as a two-and-a-half-year-old like Carter. And wondering if she would be the way he is—as happy and full of energy. Wondering if she'd say things he says, like the things he likes, *do* the things he does. Now, when I'm with Carter…" Heddy shrugged. "The Carter-isms are just the Carter-ism, and—"

Heddy took a moment to let it sink in because she

honestly was only realizing this as she said it. "Actually since being around Carter, I seem to be more able to choose when to think of Tina and in what way. It hasn't just been flooding me out of the blue the way it used to. And that's good..." It really was.

"But today, with a whole bunch of kids, and then a baby..."

"I did get blindsided by that baby," she admitted, her own low spirits beginning to lift as she talked about it all. Plus Lang was rubbing the back of her hand with his thumb and his touch actually seemed to be infusing her with some of his strength. "And when something makes me think about Tina out of the blue," she went on, "the bad feelings can still be hard." She shrugged again. "But on the other hand, today has sort of opened my eyes to how being with Carter has made things better."

"I'm not sure you're telling me the truth, but I hope so," Lang said.

Heddy managed a bigger smile. "I *am* telling you the truth," she insisted.

Lang squeezed her hand. "Still, I don't know how you got through that."

"I wasn't sure I was going to the first year," she said, finding it easier to go on talking about this now. "I don't think anyone else was too sure, either."

"Where did you live if you didn't go back to that house?"

"My parents wanted me to stay with them, but Clair wasn't married yet, and when she offered, I took her up on it. It seemed better to do that than to just go home to Mom and Dad."

"But I can't believe anything could make that situation *better*."

"No, it didn't," she confirmed. "I moved in with Clair but I was still just… I don't know, barely conscious. Clair kept me going as much as anything kept me going at the time. Too many days in bed and she'd yank me out and make me get cleaned up. She got me to eat what little I ate every day. But most of that first year I don't even remember. I just know that if it wasn't for Clair I *wouldn't* have gotten through it. And besides taking care of me, Clair hired a Realtor and got the house sold. It was Clair who got the family and movers in to pack everything, because I couldn't face any of it. I couldn't step foot in that place. It was Clair who went through every stage with me. Who was patient when I needed patience, let me cry on her shoulder and feel sorry for myself when I needed that, and gave me kicks in the pants when I needed those, too."

"And after a year? Did you just wake up on the anniversary and—"

"It's *five* years later and I've just gotten to the point where I can be around Carter," she pointed out. "No. I just sort of knew I had to try to get back to… I don't know, *something.* Clair's wedding was coming up. She was going to move into Clark's house and I had to do something with myself. Daniel had a life insurance policy—nothing huge, but it was a lump sum. And there had been some equity on the house, but I needed to get back to work."

"You didn't work that whole first year?"

She shook her head again. "I wish I could find a way to say this that didn't sound nuts, but not only couldn't

I go back to working with kids, I guess somewhere in my grief-stricken brain, I sort of associated the job—the hours, certainly, but somehow the whole thing—with Daniel and Tina dying, and blamed that."

"You think if you had been home it wouldn't have happened?" Lang asked, sounding confused.

"I know it isn't logical, but yes. Clair and the rest of my family always say that if I'd been there, I would have gone to sleep and never woken up, too. I wouldn't have been able to prevent it from happening. But still..."

"You couldn't just go on the way things had been before. Back to what you'd been doing that night. To you, one thing is connected to the other."

"Yes!" It was amazing how quickly he understood what her family had never seemed able to grasp.

"But I had to make a living."

"And that's where cheesecakes came in?"

"I'd made them before, gotten the recipes just the way I wanted them. People had always said I should sell them, so..."

"That's what you did."

"Well, I couldn't sell enough of them or you wouldn't be here, but yes."

His smile contained a hint of guilt. "And out of terrible, terrible tragedy for you came something that I'm thankful for—even though I am sorry for what you went through and all you lost," he said quietly.

Heddy acknowledged him with a small, helpless shrug.

There wasn't anything that could ever make her forget how tragic losing Daniel and Tina had been, but telling Lang had been surprisingly cathartic. And even sitting there with him, her hand still in his, felt somehow okay now, too.

Probably because he'd taken her hand simply to console her, the way any number of people had over the years, she told herself.

Although something about this wasn't quite the same…

Something about everything with Lang wasn't quite the same as it had been with anyone else she'd talked about this to.

It wasn't as if there was instantly less pain over the losses she'd suffered, or that Daniel and Tina were forgotten.

It was just that, for some reason, it all seemed to slip to the side. Into its own compartment.

Leaving her feeling…what?

She wasn't quite sure.

Daniel and Tina were still with her but she somehow felt a little freer. Freer and very aware of what was right there in front of her. For real and not just in her mind, in her memory, but in the flesh.

Lang.

He was looking down at his hand holding hers, and she was looking at his chiseled face, and for the first time the past and the present separated for her. It was as if she moved—without moving at all—more firmly into the moment.

Lang lifted her hand to look at it more closely. Then he pressed his mouth to the back of it. And unlike the night before, nothing in her shouted for her to say stop. Instead she just yearned for those lips to be on hers again.

Then he raised his blue, blue eyes to hers, searching, and she had the sense that he was torn between what he wanted and something else—knowing what he now knew about her, maybe?

Heddy couldn't be sure. But she did give in to her own inclinations to take her hand out of his so she could lay it on his cheek, so she could let him know that she was very much here in the moment with him and him alone.

At first, when he arched his brows, she wasn't sure he was convinced. But then he leaned forward and pressed his mouth to hers, kissing her tenderly, carefully, sweetly, giving her the opportunity to shove him away if he was out of line.

But Heddy didn't shove him away. She tilted her chin into that kiss and deepened it, allowing her lips to part beneath his.

Her response triggered more of a hunger in him than she'd expected, as if kissing her again was something he'd been dying to do all along. His lips parted further still, instantly turning up the heat.

He cradled her head in one hand and encircled her with his other arm, pulling her closer, holding her as his mouth opened a bit wider still, wide enough for just the tip of his tongue to tease the tip of hers.

For a split second the intimacy startled Heddy. But only for a split second. Soon she surprised herself by inviting a little play that just seemed to come naturally as the kiss enveloped her and carried her away.

She toyed with the coarse hair at the nape of his neck as their mouths opened even wider and their tongues began a dance that was more sensual than playful. Darting and enticing and circling and caressing in ways that she thought she'd forgotten how to do.

Her head resting in Lang's hand, she gave herself over to the pure strength and presence of him, to the kiss that was all-encompassing and great and glorious and so, so good that she sailed away on it and could have let it go on for hours and hours....

Except that suddenly, from somewhere very nearby, a sleepily chipper Carter said, "Wass 'at?"

Heddy had been so engrossed that she hadn't heard or even sensed Carter coming downstairs and into the living room to stand on the other side of the coffee table. Lang jolted slightly as he ended the kiss, clearly surprised, too.

But dazed and confused or not, the kiss came to an abrupt and premature end as they both glanced over at the little boy. With Baby tucked under one arm, he rubbed his eye with a balled-up fist and pointed to the plate of cookies on the coffee table with his other hand.

"Um... Those are the cookies we were having for dessert." Lang answered Carter's question foggily even as he dropped his forehead to Heddy's, silently conveying his frustration and regret that no more kissing could go on.

"I ha' one?" Carter inquired.

"Yeah. Sure. Then we should get going," Lang said before he lifted his head from Heddy's and straightened.

"He was only catnapping..." Heddy surmised.

"I guess so," Lang said on a sigh.

Then he pivoted in Carter's direction while still holding Heddy from behind.

The sleepy toddler had chosen a cookie and was eating it. "Goo' cookie," he said with his mouth full.

Heddy couldn't help smiling at the toddler in spite of the disappointment she was enduring over the end he'd put to that kiss.

But there was no going back, so instead she went forward.

Recalling something Lang had mentioned when they'd been going over the packaging, advertising and promotional material at his office, she said, "There was some P.R. thing you wanted to talk to me about?"

Lang took a deep breath and sighed again, clearly—but only reluctantly—yielding to their new circumstances.

"Right. I did," he said stoically. Then, when he seemed to get his bearings, he went on. "Saturday night there's a charity event at the Denver Country Club."

"The big leagues," Heddy joked.

"It's an auction, and I was thinking that if you spent the rest of this week baking the way you did for your shop—at Camden Inc.'s expense, not out of your own pocket—we could donate all the cheesecakes to that."

"The list of things to be auctioned off isn't already set this close to the event?"

He grinned sheepishly. "I can pull a few strings."

The Camden name. And probably long-standing membership.

"Anyway," he continued, "I thought we could have small sample bites for bidders to taste to whet their appetites, and contribute the full-size cheesecakes to the auction. Part of it will be silent, so people can bid on each cheesecake separately."

"I was wondering if you were thinking of having open bidding, one cheesecake at a time. But sure, I can see how a silent auction would work—people could vie for the one they particularly like, I suppose."

"There'll be news coverage of the event itself and I'll make sure the cheesecakes are mentioned. We'll get people tasting them, buying them and feeding them to their friends. And we can announce that it will all be for sale at Camden Superstores before long."

Heddy had been dreading the downtime of the shop being closed. "I think that's a great idea," she told him.

"Now for the second part..."

"It's twofold?"

"I think we should make an appearance along with the cheesecakes so I can introduce you around."

Heddy laughed as if he were kidding.

But he wasn't.

"You want me to attend a charity auction at the Denver Country Club?" she said.

"With me right by your side every minute, if the thought freaks you out."

"Oh, it definitely freaks me out."

Carter had finished his cookie and was reaching for a second one, but Lang got up in a hurry and snatched the little boy before he could. "Let's get your coat on," he said. As he got Carter ready, he glanced at Heddy again and went on talking about Saturday night.

"It's casual dress—not tuxes and formal gowns. I'll wear a suit, and any dress you have would do just fine. And I *promise* you, I won't leave you on your own for even a minute. My sister Livi is keeping Carter overnight—her one exception to the I-have-to-do-everything-with-him-on-my-own rule—so it will only be the two of us, and I will make absolutely sure that there isn't a single minute that you feel uncomfortable."

"'Nother cookie," Carter demanded once his coat was on and zipped up.

"How about if I put them in a bag and send them home with you?" Heddy asked as she considered what Lang was suggesting.

It *was* just business, she told herself.

Business that would get her into the Denver Country Club on a Saturday night. With him.

But still, just business…

"Will the other contributors to the auction be there, too?" she asked.

"Most of the donations are made by members, so sure."

Members, not people getting grants from members.

"Come on," Lang cajoled as if he could tell she was having doubts. "There will be cocktails and a nice dinner. You'll meet a few people and get to see some cutthroat bidding by some of the members who are always competing with each other. Crazy things get auctioned off and even crazier amounts get paid for them. It'll be fun."

She believed that because she suspected that he would go out of his way to make sure of it.

And it *was* business. Not a date. If it were a date that would be something else. But this was to help launch the new avenue of her career.

"It sounds like a dirty job but if someone has to do it…" Heddy finally conceded.

"Great!" With Carter slung on his hip and the three

of them headed for the back door, Lang leaned close to Heddy's ear and said, "I can't tell you how much I can use a night off!"

Heddy laughed at him.

"Go to our store on Ralston Road and ask for Ed—he manages it. I'll let him know that you have carte blanche. Get everything you need and he'll send me the bill. Then bake your little heart out and whatever you end up with is what we'll donate. I'll have one of our refrigerated trucks pick them up on Saturday and take them over to the club."

"Okay," Heddy agreed as they reached the door.

Carter had laid his head wearily on Lang's broad shoulder and was drifting off again, clutching Baby and the plastic baggy of cookies. Heddy opened the door for them to go out.

But Lang only made it midway across the threshold before he stopped to peer down at her in a way that told her business was behind them again and this moment was purely personal.

"I want you to know," he said in a voice that was for her ears alone, "that even before what you told me tonight, I thought you were really something. Now I know it. You've been through more than I can imagine and you're still standing—without any guards up that I've seen. That isn't something I can say even about myself."

It was Heddy's turn to be confused but now wasn't the time to explore what he'd said.

Anyway, before she could, he added, "I admire that. And you…"

He bent and kissed her again, solidly, soundly, with

the intimacy from earlier just around the edges to remind her.

"I'll talk to you this week," he said when the kiss ended and he stepped outside into the night.

Heddy closed the door after him, the feel of his mouth on hers still fresh and more wonderful than she wanted to admit.

But even as she indulged for a moment in reliving this kiss and the much hotter one earlier, something else crept in.

She remembered the feeling that had come over her after she'd told Lang about Daniel and Tina. The feeling that it had all slipped to the side just a little. That she was somehow just a little more free…

And without understanding how or why, she knew that she'd turned a corner.

A corner she hadn't thought she would ever be able to turn.

But for some reason, she had.

Tonight.

In just that one moment.

With Lang.

## *Chapter Seven*

"What does the zoo have to do with cheesecakes?" Clair asked.

Heddy's cousin had dropped in on Friday to find Heddy on her way out. After not seeing or hearing from Lang on Tuesday, Wednesday or Thursday, he had called that morning. It was one of April's perfect spring days and he'd decided to leave work at two o'clock to take Carter to the zoo. He said that he thought Heddy deserved a break, too, and he'd invited her to meet them at his house to go with them.

Eager to see him again after three days of thinking almost nonstop about him, Heddy had ignored all the reasons why she should decline and had agreed.

But now Clair had dropped in. And while Clair was supportive of taking the grant from the Camdens and selling cheesecakes through Camden Superstores—especially since Clark had given the legal go-ahead—

she was clearly leery of Heddy spending an afternoon at the zoo with Lang Camden.

And Heddy hadn't even told her cousin about the kissing. She was still struggling with guilt over it and couldn't bring herself to talk about it.

"The zoo doesn't have anything to do with cheesecakes," she said in answer to Clair's question. "It's just a beautiful day and Lang thought I might like to go. No big deal."

"Unless it is..." Clair said ominously. "I saw him, remember? He's the kind of man women leave their husbands for. He's a gorgeous hunk of rich, charming masculinity, and if he's trying to sweep you off your feet—"

Was he?

"No. I don't think he's trying to sweep mc off my feet by asking me to go to thc zoo."

"I wouldn't want you to fall into the same trap your mom fell into."

They were standing in Heddy's kitchen while Heddy checked her purse to make sure she had her wallet, her keys and everything she might need for a two-and-a-half-year-old at the zoo in case Lang didn't think ahead.

But when she zipped up her well-stocked purse she didn't sling the strap over her shoulder to leave. Instead she leaned back against the edge of the counter behind her, looked at Clair and thought about what her cousin had said.

*Was* she falling into the same trap her mother had?

"It doesn't seem like Lang is setting any kind of trap," shc said.

"But you're falling anyway?" Clair observed with alarm in her voice.

"No, I'm not *falling* for him," Heddy insisted. "But something *has* happened...."

"Something like what?"

Heddy tried to describe what had happened to her on Monday night. She didn't tell her cousin about the kissing. She only told her about the realizations she'd come to about finding it easier to be around Carter now, and how therapeutic it had been to tell Lang about Daniel and Tina.

"I mean, sure, Carter is a cute kid and maybe that helped reboot me a little when it comes to kids. I guess that isn't so hard to figure out. But the other..."

She shook her head, still perplexed by what had come over her. "I don't know... It isn't as if I haven't talked about Daniel and Tina and what happened a million times before to you and the rest of the family and my friends and Daniel's friends and... Well, you know."

Clair nodded.

"But for some reason this time..." Heddy shrugged. "I just ended up feeling...I don't know, as if once it was out I'd passed some kind of point that let me feel better in general. I can't explain it. Maybe there's some magic number of times to talk about it and once I'd hit it—"

"*That* would be great. But if there isn't a magic number and you feel better because of Lang Camden, because you're attracted to him, and telling him about Daniel put it behind you and opened the way to this guy—*that* worries me."

"It wasn't like I put it *behind* me," Heddy hedged. "It

will always be a part of me. Daniel and Tina will always be a part of me."

Clair cut to the chase. "I just don't want to see you get hurt, Heddy. After Daniel and Tina and the past five years. If you get hurt on your first time out of the gate… That scares me. And the Camden track record with Hanrahan women isn't good."

"Yeah, it's *horrible,*" Heddy confirmed.

And maybe, she thought, Clair was her wake-up call today. Maybe she *had* slightly lost sight of the history between the Camdens and the Hanrahans. And she needed not to do that.

Even if, for whatever reason, she was beginning to emerge from the dark space she'd been in for the past five years, that didn't change the situation. Lang was still a Camden. She was still doing business with him. And yes, when it came to personal relationships between Camdens and Hanrahans, the Camdens most certainly did have a well-earned bad reputation.

"It's okay," she said resolutely then. "It's gotten a little personal with Lang. He's easy to talk to. He makes me laugh. And yes, I'll admit that I haven't hated being with him—he's been a good time-filler."

But she wasn't going to admit to more than that. She wasn't going to tell her cousin that she was having trouble *not* thinking about him when she wasn't with him, that she hoped he was on the other end of the line every time her phone rang, or on the other side of the door whenever someone stopped by. And she wasn't going to tell her cousin about the kissing. Or how much she'd liked it. How much she found herself craving more of it.

No, she needed to put a stop to all of that and she

knew it, so why confess to what was already over and done with—what she was going to make sure didn't happen again? It would only cause Clair to worry more.

Instead she said, "It isn't as if this is a relationship or anything. It's not like Mom planning her future with Mitchum Camden and waiting for the engagement ring that never came. Being with Lang right now is just temporary while he helps me get things going."

That had come out sounding different than she'd intended it to. Maybe because there were a lot of things that Lang was helping her to get going again.

"While he helps me get things going with the new business," she amended. "And pays the bills through the grant. But I don't have any illusions. Once I'm up and running, I won't even see or hear from him again. I'll deal with a Camden Superstore purchaser or something."

"But today you're going to the zoo with him," Clair said as if she wanted to be convinced but still had her doubts.

"It's just the zoo. And every time we've been together it's really about business. He probably wants to talk about logos and packaging, or about what I'll need to do at the charity auction tomorrow night to promote the cheesecakes. And there's always Carter—I'm not alone with Lang."

Well, she would be tomorrow night at the charity auction. And not being alone hadn't stopped what had happened so far.

But she opted not to tell her cousin those things, either.

"Just be careful, okay?" Clair said. "Don't be thinking that you're immune because of Daniel and Tina, that this guy *can't* get to you. Because if anyone could, it might be him."

There was truth in that.

"It's okay. My mom is cautionary tale enough," Heddy assured her as she and Clair went out the back door to their respective cars.

Clair still looked worried as they parted ways but as Heddy got behind the wheel and headed for Cherry Creek she was still thinking that her mother was definitely a cautionary tale that she had every intention of heeding.

Yes, it was a little nice that for the first time in five years she had twinges of excitement over the thought of seeing someone.

But that's all it was—just a *little* nice.

A little nice and a little heartening to discover that she might not be as dead inside as she'd thought.

She didn't have any illusions, though.

This was what it was.

In the first place, it was just for now. And if this was the beginning of a reawakening for her, good. But there wasn't anything else to it. She wasn't hanging any hopes—high or otherwise—on it the way her mother had with Mitchum Camden. She wasn't clutching to it like a lifeline. She wasn't even looking at it as a replacement for anything.

Because Daniel and Tina couldn't be replaced, and she certainly had no desire to try.

This was just something that was happening for the moment. It was setting the stage for her financial future, and it was possibly giving her a sign that there might be life after Daniel in some form or another. Somewhere far, far down the road. Someday.

And not with Lang Camden.

But for now this was the best she'd felt in the past five years and she just couldn't help enjoying it.

Cautiously, now that Clair had delivered the wake-up call.

But some just the same.

"Immuh chark. You goss a hot dog for me?" Carter asked Heddy, interrupting the hellos Heddy and Lang had only begun to exchange.

"At the zoo, Carter. I told you, I'll get you a hot dog at the zoo," Lang said.

Heddy was sitting in the passenger seat of Lang's SUV en route to the Denver Zoo that was only blocks from his house. She'd called to let him know she was running late, and he had been putting Carter in the car seat when she'd arrived so she'd gone directly from her car to his.

In response to what she knew must be a quizzical expression on her face, Lang explained Carter's greeting. "He's a shark."

"Ah! I was wondering what he had on," Heddy said.

"My cousin Jani took him to the aquarium one day when she was babysitting for me and bought him the shark suit. He decides out of the blue that he's a *chark* and he *has* to wear it. As for the hot dog—he's been asking for one of those since I let him put on the suit and I've been telling him he could have one at the zoo, but he's still asked every single person he's seen—all day long—if they have a hot dog for him."

Heddy laughed, taking a closer look at Carter over the corner of the seat.

The shark suit he was wearing was probably intended to be a Halloween costume. He was covered head to toe in what could have passed for a lightly padded gray snowsuit with his face peeking out from the shark's mouth, surrounded like a sunflower by felt shark teeth.

"I goss eyes," Carter told her when he saw her studying him. He swiveled as much as his car seat restraints allowed to show her the plastic shark eyes on the back of the hood.

"You do have shark eyes," she answered. Then to Lang she said, "The suit keeps him from needing a coat."

"I figured the same thing. Sixty degrees is nice, but he still would have had to wear a jacket." Lang cast her a grin and added, "And he is funny in it."

"Especially since he thinks sharks eat hot dogs," Heddy said, glad to see that he found the situation humorous.

"Yeah, I have no idea where the hot dog thing comes in."

Once they arrived at the zoo and parked, Heddy went around to the driver's side to wait for Lang to take Carter out of his car seat.

Lang must have changed since he'd left the office because he wasn't dressed for work now. He was wearing a navy blue Henley sweater and a pair of jeans that fitted him to perfection.

To such perfection that when he leaned into the car door opening, her eyes got stuck on his rear end and she could barely tear them away when he came out of the SUV with Carter in tow.

"See? Immuh chark!" Carter felt the need to repeat once Lang had set him on his feet and the two-and-a-half-year-old could show Heddy the fin and tail down the back of his suit.

"You really are," Heddy confirmed.

Then Carter surprised her by taking her hand as they went up to the gates.

She'd never had the chance to take Tina to the zoo, and the thought weighed heavily on Heddy's mind as she walked with Carter through the first few exhibits. A sadness she was only too familiar with came on board and with it thoughts about Daniel and wishes that she'd had a day like today with her husband and child.

But being with Carter and Lang helped diminish her sadness before long, allowing her to begin to enjoy herself.

How could she not as she watched the innocent mischief of Carter chasing a goose or trying unsuccessfully to climb the safety fences in his shark suit, or his unbridled glee over the real-life "Zsorzses" swinging from trees in the monkey house?

His joy was infectious, and having Lang beside her, making jokes and funny remarks about Carter and his antics, helped her to let the day be only about Carter and how delighted he was with every aspect of their trip to the zoo.

In fact, it was so infectious that she actually found herself having glimmers of the child Tina might have been and *didn't* suffer for it.

"I wanna hot dog," Carter reminded them petulantly as they drove away from the zoo.

"I can't believe I couldn't find him a hot dog," Lang

muttered to Heddy. "How do you feel about having those for dinner?"

Heddy hadn't known she was expected to have dinner with them.

But before she could say so, Lang said, "You will have dinner with us, won't you? I brought home the mock-ups for the changes we asked for on the logo and since you drove all the way over here to go to the zoo with us, I was hoping you'd let me buy you dinner. I thought maybe pizza because, you know—" He nodded toward Carter. "But now, can I persuade you to have a hot dog and then we can check the new logo?"

"Sure."

"Great! Because I don't think there's any chance we're getting the chark to eat anything else. So how about I stop at the store and run in real quick to get everything, then we'll go back to my place, feed the chark, I'll put him to bed and we can check out the logos?"

"Okay," Heddy agreed, glad that even that much business was going to be done.

Because so far today, there hadn't been any business the way she'd assured her cousin there would be.

Lang cooked hot dogs on the grill in the center of a stove that nearly made Heddy drool with envy. Carter ate his hot dog plain with ketchup, but Lang and Heddy spruced theirs up with chili, cheese and mustard. Potato chips rounded out the meal that was hardly fancy but delicious nevertheless, and then Heddy offered to clean up while Lang bathed Carter and put him to bed.

The kitchen was barely messy, so once Heddy had thrown away their paper plates and napkins and washed off the countertops, she had a chance to take a closer look at the state-of-the-art space and appliances.

It seemed like vast overkill for a man who claimed not to cook but to Heddy it was a dream kitchen. The overall color scheme was pristine white with touches of gray, the floor was tiled, the counters were all marble and the appliances were top-of-the-line stainless steel. The space was larger than Heddy's kitchen, dining and living areas combined.

But the entire house seemed like overkill for a single man, even one with a recently inherited child.

Lang had dispatched Carter to show her around while he'd cooked and to Heddy's surprise, the two-and-a-half-year-old had taken the job seriously. He'd again grabbed her hand and proved to be quite the tour guide.

The house was a two-story with four bedrooms and four bathrooms upstairs. On the ground floor there was a den, a family room, a living room and formal dining room to go along with the kitchen. There were two additional bathrooms on the lower level, and yet another one in the finished basement, which Heddy hadn't had a chance to see before dinner was ready. But she had no doubt that the "playroom" and the "potty" Carter told her were downstairs were equally as impressive as the rest of the place.

After a few minutes, Lang still hadn't come back downstairs, so Heddy slipped into the guest bathroom to see how she'd fared after her day at the zoo.

Not too badly, she decided, since her red turtleneck sweater and jeans were unmarred.

She had her hair swept back loosely so it was full but contained. Even though a few wisps had escaped to curl around her face, it hadn't gone too wild so she just left them. Especially when she heard the sound of footsteps descending the stairs.

Slipping out of the bathroom, she went into the kitchen again just as Lang entered from the back stairway.

"Okay, he's down for the count!" he announced. "Now for *our* dessert."

Why did there seem to be a sexual undertone in that?

Maybe she was just imagining it, she thought as Lang went to the freezer and took out a large tub of ice cream.

"Sweet Action," he said, this time distinctly putting a sensual spin to the words. "Have you had it?" he asked, his innuendo clearly intentional because he raised a roguish eyebrow at her.

"Is that the kind of ice cream?" she asked, nodding toward the name on the label on the side of the tub and not giving him any satisfaction.

"It is," he confirmed. "The best ice cream in the world. Especially when I top it..."

Both eyebrows wiggled salaciously then and Heddy couldn't help laughing at him.

"Do you always get this worked up over ice cream?" she asked.

"Wait until you taste it. And what I do with it..."

Heddy laughed at him again and watched as he spooned out the praline ice cream and then poured a praline liqueur over the top.

One bite and Heddy forgave him his innuendos. "That *is* wonderful!"

"And you thought you were the only one who could do divine desserts," he chided, practically gloating.

Then he suggested they take their ice cream and sit in the living room to look at the logos.

Neither of them had liked the advertising department's first very contemporary design, but now a French twist had been given to the lettering and there was an Eiffel Tower logo to denote that cheesecake had its origin in French cuisine. After looking over the material spread out on Lang's glass coffee table, they agreed that was the way to go.

Then they sat back, both of them near the center of the comfortable overstuffed white leather sofa, angled to face each other.

And Heddy decided to let some of her curiosity have free rein.

"This is a beautiful house," she began.

"Thanks."

"But not where I pictured you living. It's not really a bachelor pad."

His smile was wry. "Yeah, it wasn't intended to be a bachelor pad."

"It's a great family home. Did you buy it after you found out that Carter was yours?"

"No, I bought it four years ago. It was a surprise. And a Hail Mary play."

"A Hail Mary play?"

"In football it's a desperation play, and that's what buying this house was for me. I was engaged and having trouble getting my fiancée to the altar."

He finished his ice cream and set the bowl on the coffee table next to the logos.

Heddy had finished hers, too, and did the same. She had the sense that he wasn't eager to talk about this but since he'd said that much she ventured a little further anyway.

"Was that the relationship you spun out of before you met Carter's mom?"

"It was," he confirmed on a sigh. "My first girlfriend. My first date. My first love. My first everything."

"Ah, the all-important First."

"Was your husband that for you?"

Heddy shook her head. "I met Daniel in college, so there had been a few boyfriends before that. Nothing serious—just teenage dating stuff, dances and what-have-you. Daniel was my first..." and only lover. But now that she'd started to say it she didn't know how to finish, so she altered her course and said, "When I met Daniel I knew almost instantly that he was who I was meant to be with."

"I know that feeling."

"Daniel always said he felt the same way," Heddy offered, hurting a little even as she recalled it.

"Audrey didn't," Lang said. "She didn't say it and I'm sure now that she never felt it."

Heddy hurt a little more for him. "That's her name? Audrey?"

"Audrey Vincent. We met in ninth grade. We were both fourteen and we were inseparable from then on—weird as that seems now that I know what I know."

"My aunt and uncle—Clair's mom and dad—started going together when they were thirteen and never stopped, and they've lived happily ever after, so it's not so strange."

"Yeah, living happily ever after—that's how I imagined it would be with Audrey. We were together all through high school, went to college together in Fort Collins and moved in together after college, which is when I asked her to marry me."

"You called her your fiancée, so she must have said yes."

"She did. Without hesitation." There was a hint of disillusionment in his tone. "It was just after that that things… I don't know. They *seemed* the same. But whenever I'd want to set a wedding date, she'd put me off. For two and a half years."

"Was she busy getting her career started?" Heddy asked.

"She had a trust fund, plus I didn't care if she worked at all, so no. She did work a few days a week in one of her father's car dealerships, but it wasn't anything she was devoted to. I would have understood something like that. But we were basically settled into mock-married life—she just wouldn't take that last step to make it genuine married life." He seemed lost for a moment in memories. Then he looked at Heddy and said, "How long were you engaged before you got married?"

"Daniel proposed at the end of our freshman year of college. We were married the next November," she admitted, hoping it didn't make him feel worse.

"So basically a six-month engagement?"

That seemed to put his two and a half years to shame so, implying that they'd been impulsive, Heddy said, "We were really young."

"And how long were you married?" Lang asked.

"Five years. Our parents didn't want us to get married until after college but we wanted to have a few years alone together before we started a family. And we wanted to start our family by the time we were both twenty-five."

"And you had a three-month-old by the time you were twenty-five, so you were right on schedule," Lang said as if he envied that.

"Then life hit me with a curve," she reminded him, hoping to let him know he wasn't the only one for whom something important hadn't worked out.

"I guess I'd have to say that it was Audrey who hit me with a curve. After being engaged for so long I wanted to push forward, so I bought this place," he said, getting back to what had begun this subject. "It came on the market all of a sudden and Audrey was familiar with the house—one of her friends had grown up here and she loved the place. I decided to surprise her with it, figured we'd celebrate by finally setting a date."

That seemed like such a wonderful surprise. This beautiful house and a gorgeous, charming guy really wanting to get married… What was wrong with that woman? Heddy wondered. But she didn't say it.

Instead she asked, "But it didn't happen like that?"

"What it did was push her to the point of telling me that for a long time she'd liked the idea that I loved her more than she loved me."

"Oh." Heddy said, trying to imagine what she would have felt if Daniel had said that to her. And hurting again for Lang.

"It seemed so… At first I thought she was kidding," he said, sounding stunned even now. "Maybe it's male vanity or ego that caused me to miss something, but until she said that, I'd believed we felt the same way about each other."

"When you look back, were there any signs that she didn't?"

He shrugged. "She'd never cheated or even talked about wanting to date other people. She'd moved in with me. She'd said yes to the proposal. I guess maybe I might have been the first one of us to say the I-love-yous a lot of the time…" He shrugged again.

"But that night here…" he continued.

He shook his head and Heddy watched the emotions cross his handsome face.

"Audrey said she just didn't love me enough to spend her whole life with me. That she'd been struggling with it, trying to feel more than she did, hoping it would come in time, but it just didn't and she didn't think it ever would."

For a moment silence fell. Lang's gaze was off in the distance. Then he shook his head again and shrugged once more before refocusing on Heddy.

"That was it," he said with finality. "She gave me back the ring, moved out of the loft we were living in and I haven't seen her since." There was lingering shock in his tone.

Heddy recalled something he'd said when she'd told him about Daniel and Tina. "But it hit you hard."

"Oh yeah," he admitted. "First there was the wallowing part. Then there was the anger part. Then there was the partying like there was no tomorrow and meeting Carter's mother—"

"And then you came to grips with it all but it had changed you," Heddy concluded.

"Yeah," he acknowledged. "Audrey left me knowing that I'll never let myself be all-in unless I know damn good and well that the other person is all-in, too. Of course that isn't how my family interprets the change in me. They think I shut myself off, that I keep people at arm's length since Audrey."

The kisses they'd shared popped into Heddy's mind. She certainly hadn't felt as if he'd kept her at arm's length.

"They think I've built a wall around myself," he added.

"But you don't think they're right?" she asked, hearing doubt in his tone.

He seemed to consider his answer before he said, "I think I've become careful."

"Understandably."

"I think I might have kept things a little superficial with everyone I've been with since Audrey." His brows pulled together for a moment before he amended that. "Well, with almost everyone. Lately I'm beginning to wonder if *that* isn't changing a little."

*With me?*

Heddy thought she had to be wrong in wondering that.

But he *was* looking at her with a warmth that hadn't been in his blue eyes while he'd talked about his past.

"I don't know," he said then. "We're all products of what we've been through, and *something* changes in us along the way. Maybe it changes pretty drastically in the recoil then relaxes a little so we end up somewhere between where we were at both extremes. But we're still changed to some extent."

Which was true for her. She'd been able to do things with Carter and Lang that she hadn't been able to bring herself to do for the past five years. But she still had some reservations….

Lang smiled and stretched an arm along the sofa back, pushing a wisp of her hair from the side of her face with an index finger. "I guess we can't swing completely back to the naive happiness because we're weighed down with what I believe is considered *baggage*."

"So what does that make this house? Your deluxe leather steamer trunk?"

He grinned and glanced around as if he honestly did like the place. "Yeah, this isn't too shabby a piece of baggage to have ended up with," he agreed. "It took me a while to decide whether or not to keep it. But in order to improve my investment it needed remodeling and updating. Once the work was finished, and I'd picked everything out, it felt like mine. So I moved in. I guess you could say it's the something-not-too-shabby that came out of the ugly. Kind of like your cheesecakes—although it seems like I got a bigger not-too-shabby out of a smaller ugly, and you kind of got a smaller not-too-shabby out of a bigger ugly."

The way he put it made her smile. "I certainly hope my cheesecakes are *not too shabby*."

But it was definitely not too shabby to have him stroking the side of her face, which was what he'd started to do after moving her hair aside.

"And now here we are," he said in a lower, more intimate voice, "maybe the worse for wear but still kicking just the same."

"To our credit?" she said, thinking more about how he'd recovered from what his fiancée had said and done to him than about herself.

She sat there peering into his eyes, somehow seeing even more depth in them, in him, now. She knew he was a Camden and that her mother put all Camdens into the same category of cad, but Heddy couldn't help feeling that Lang was a good man.

He leaned forward enough to kiss her then, catching her midthought so she didn't see it coming. But it didn't matter because unlike when he'd kissed her by surprise before, this time she just instinctively kissed him back.

She wasn't supposed to be doing that, she reminded herself. And since she hadn't prevented it from happening again—the way she'd sworn she would—she knew she should at least try to break it off now.

But he had such terrific lips—warm and just soft enough…

And he was so talented at using them; parting them the perfect amount, positioning them over hers just right.

Plus he smelled divinely of the lightest, cleanest cologne.

And he tasted of the praline liqueur, sweet and heady.

And she just plain liked kissing him.

So she did. She went on kissing him, telling herself she'd only do it for a bit. Because how could she reject him when she'd just heard how horribly that silly, silly other woman had?

He cradled her head in his hand as he brought his other arm around to pull her closer, and she went willingly. Willingly and fully aware that no matter how she rationalized it, she was surrendering just because she ached to be held by him, to be up against that big, broad-shouldered body.

They opened their mouths wider and tongues met

with vigor as thoughts of everything and everyone floated from Heddy's mind and she drifted away on the pure sensations of being so thoroughly kissed by Lang once more.

She raised her hands to his chest—rock-hard and muscular—and wished that his sweater was thinner, that there wasn't quite so much fabric between her palms and him. Wished that there might be nothing at all between them....

But she chased that thought from her mind the minute it appeared there, reminding herself that she wasn't even supposed to be kissing him.

And kissing him and kissing him and kissing him.

There was more zeal to it than there had been before, more heat, more hunger. So much more that Heddy's nipples became tiny knots and other things—long-sleeping things—slowly, lazily, began to awaken inside her.

And suddenly she was aware of not just an inclination to have her hands on him, but of an even stronger inclination to have his hands on her.

It was as if her breasts had a mind of their own and somehow swelled into closer contact with his chest.

But her hands were in the way.

So she slid them around him, to the wide expanse of his back, her fingers splaying against him and doing their own part in bringing her near enough so that her oh-so-tight nipples brushed his chest.

He released her hair from its clip to fall free for the first time since she'd met him. Then he threaded both hands through the long strands at the back of her head, holding it steady against an even deeper onslaught of kisses that were rapidly intensifying and feeding the need in Heddy for even more.

She found the hem of Lang's sweater and snaked her fingers under it to finally reach skin. Warm, satin-over-steel skin.

And just when she was thinking that nothing had ever felt so good to her before, he took her lead and trailed one of his hands to the bottom of her sweater, slipping it underneath.

Goose bumps erupted all along the surface of her skin at that first touch and she nearly shivered with delight. Like the first sip of water after a long, long draught, she drank in the feel of a man's hands on her—even just on her back—and ached for even more.

Their tongues were doing a fevered dance as Heddy explored every mound of muscle in Lang's back, massaging and memorizing the tone and texture of it all, while he gave hers a very, very fine massage as well, holding her even tighter to him.

His hand on her back felt huge and strong and powerful and incredibly, incredibly good, turning her insides to mush and making her yearn for him to touch her breasts in the same way.

As if he could hear her thoughts, his hand veered off course, coming from her back to her waist, then moving upward along her side, closer and closer to her breast....

She pulled her shoulders back, extending an invitation. An invitation that he took, bringing his hand forward and finding just one of the two parts of her that craved his attention.

But he only touched her on the outside of the bra that she willed to just disappear.

He did the next best thing, though: he snuck a hand in under the band and finally gave her what she wanted, what she wanted more than she knew until she got it—the wonders of his bare hand on her bare breast.

A tiny half sigh, half moan escaped from her throat as the sumptuousness of that sensation set in, as he cupped her breast in his palm and pressed his fingers tenderly into her soft flesh.

Her nipple was a tight knot in the center of his palm, asserting itself there as he began to work magic. Then he found it with gentle fingertips that carefully pinched and pulled and circled, and took her up another level of desire, of need.

He didn't neglect her other breast, giving equal attention there. Equal pleasure. And melting Heddy from the inside out as their mouths continued to play a sensuous game.

And still she wanted more. Just when she was enmeshed in the wonders of his touch, she somehow started to think of tearing his sweater off. Of tearing her own sweater off. Of being skin-to-skin with him. Everywhere. Because yes, she went on to think about jeans flying. About being able to see for herself if he looked as great out of clothes as he looked in them. If he looked as great as he felt…

It was only the thought of being naked herself that made a twinge of inhibition rear its head, keeping her from actually tearing off his sweater.

It was a very brightly lit living room. And while that made it all the better to see him, the thought of being seen herself gave her pause.

And into that pause came a little sanity, too.

And the reminder that she had promised herself that she wouldn't even kiss him tonight.

A promise she'd made for good reason.

Yes, Lang had been instrumental in showing her that she really had moved through some of her grief. It was a huge step to find herself able to be attracted to him. So attracted to him that, yes, there was a part of her wanting to just let herself go.

But to allow that attraction to get out of hand?

The newly sane part of her made her ask herself if she wanted her story to be that after five years of grieving she'd followed in her mother's footsteps by falling for a Camden, only to have him leave her in his dust?

The answer, of course, was no.

And exactly what Heddy had sworn wouldn't happen because she wouldn't put herself in that position.

In *this* position—in Lang's arms, more and more of her turning to jelly with every minute that their kiss went on, that his hands were on her breasts…

And as much as she wanted it to continue, it was sanity that prevailed and she knew she couldn't let it.

Maybe for just another minute…

For just another minute she kissed him with all her might. She let her breasts nestle into his hand, absorbing every feeling, every thrill, savoring it all.

For just another minute she let herself have this moment, this experience, with this man….

But even though another minute became another minute and she still wanted another minute, she forced some control.

"Okay… No… We shouldn't be doing this," she whispered in a ragged voice when she'd ended the kiss.

He dropped his forehead to the top of her head. "I know…" he said as he slowly, firmly dragged the heel of his hand across one nipple and nearly drove her out of her mind.

But then he took that hand from under her bra and sweater, and rested it on her thigh.

"I'm gonna go," Heddy said then, not wanting to give any more explanation or detail, not wanting to have to tell him that if he wasn't a Camden this might have ended differently. Because certainly everything inside her was shouting for her to stay and let things reach their full and fully satisfying climax.

But Lang didn't ask any questions. He tugged her sweater firmly down around her hips, straightened away from her, then took her hand and helped her to her feet.

Without another word he walked her to his front door and held her coat for her. Then, leaving the front door open, he took her hand again as he walked her to her car.

It was there—only once he'd opened her car door for her and stood with it between them—that he leaned over and kissed her again. A long, lingering kiss that made her want to rush back inside and finish this after all.

But before she came too close to doing that, he brought the kiss to a conclusion and said, "The auction tomorrow night—"

"I'll be here at seven," Heddy confirmed what they'd discussed earlier.

Then she got into her car and started the engine, putting it into gear while Lang studied her as if he were applying every detail of her to memory before he finally closed the door.

Heddy waved goodbye, aching for the touch of the hand he waved back at her.

Then she pulled out of his driveway and headed home.

Thinking as she did about how near she'd just come to making love with someone who wasn't Daniel.

And surprising herself by somehow actually *not* feeling guilty about that.

She thought the guilt would probably come. Like an aftershock.

But right then it wasn't there.

Not even when she realized just how much she still wanted to be with Lang, actually making love....

## *Chapter Eight*

"Look at you! Woo-hoo!"

"Woo-hoo!" Carter hooted, parroting his aunt Livi, who was there to pick him up so Lang and Heddy could attend the country club's charity auction.

"Go get your coat, Carter," Lang instructed, as the toddler climbed the stairs to his room, chanting, "Woo-hoo. Woo-hoo. Woo-hoo."

When the woo-hoos reached the top of the steps and died down, Lang responded to his sister's comment. "The suit looks okay? I wasn't sure it would still fit."

"Does that suit look *okay?* Is that really what you're asking? It looks better than okay. I just can't believe you're finally wearing it and not for—"

"Don't say it," Lang warned.

"Audrey," Livi said anyway.

"The suit wasn't *for* Audrey," Lang claimed.

Although he had had it custom-made in Italy at the

cost of a small car for their honeymoon in Monte Carlo. The honeymoon that he'd also planned to surprise Audrey with. The honeymoon that had never happened. So the suit had never been worn beyond trying it on at the demand of his sisters when it had arrived from Milan.

"It might not have been *for* Audrey, but you still haven't worn it *because* of Audrey," Livi pointed out. "And it's a shame because now that I see it again I can tell you that it was almost worth what it cost you. It's one of the most beautiful suits I've ever seen."

Gray wool with the tiniest fleck of black in the fabric. Faultlessly tailored and worn over the custom-made shirt and tie that were both white, the tie with similar flecks of black in it.

"So-oo…is something going on with Heddy Hanrahan?" Livi asked, the suit obviously having raised her suspicions.

"Just because I'm wearing this suit? Come on," Lang said as if his sister was out of her mind to even think that.

When, of course, it was true that *something* was going on with Heddy. He just wasn't too sure exactly *what.*

But he wasn't going to tell his sister so he stuck with denial.

"We're doing business, remember?" Lang said. "It would be out of line for anything else to be going on."

"That didn't stop Dad and her mom…."

"And look how that ended. That's why we're helping her—to make up for that. You think I want Carter to have to be doing that for me thirty years from now?"

Livi didn't look convinced.

"And don't forget Carter," he added, citing the second

of three absolutely valid reasons for him to resist his attraction to Heddy. "I've blundered into fatherhood, I'm blundering *as* a father. The last thing I need right now is to get personally involved with anyone. I'm barely keeping my head above water as it is."

"You're doing fine with Carter," Livi argued. "Better every time I see the two of you."

"Still, would you choose *now* to fix me up with someone, even if she was the most perfect woman?" Which Heddy actually seemed to be, even though he kept trying to discover some flaw—*any* flaw—that might help him resist what was growing between them.

"No," Livi admitted. "You're doing well with Carter, but it *is* Carter you need to be bonding with. This *wouldn't* be the right time to start a relationship with a woman."

Regardless of how kind and gorgeous and warm she was. Regardless of the fact that he was thinking about her every minute, dying to be with her whenever he wasn't and actually physically aching for her.

Things that hadn't happened to him since Audrey.

Which was the third of his very real reasons to shut down what seemed to be developing on its own with Heddy. He wouldn't ever again risk going through the kind of agony he'd been left with over Audrey. And what were the odds of Heddy going for a Camden? Lousy, that's what they were.

He just didn't know what to do to stop things with Heddy.

"But you *are* wearing that suit," Livi reminded him, as if that fact contradicted all his objections.

"I'm wearing the suit because it caught my eye when

I was standing in the closet, and for the first time..." He shrugged. "Hell, Liv, I don't know. For the first time I wanted to wear it. I didn't care about the rest."

Although he *had* wanted to wear it because he was going to be with Heddy.

Livi's expression showed surprise. "You didn't care that the suit was for your honeymoon or about the whole Audrey deal? That's a big step," she said. "And a really good sign."

Was it a good sign? Because Lang wasn't sure. It was unsettling to find something—some*one*—trumping Audrey in any way.

"It means that you're finally—*really*—getting over Audrey," Livi continued.

"I've been over Audrey for a long time," he insisted, knowing it was true but understanding that his family didn't believe it. His approach with women since Audrey was like adding a security alarm after a break-in—a safety precaution to keep himself from going through the same thing twice. To keep history from repeating itself.

What he didn't understand was why Heddy Hanrahan seemed to be the exception when he wasn't willing to make an exception.

"Whatever," Livi said, making her own opinion obvious. "I'm just so glad to see you in that suit and thrilled to know that you *don't* care about any of the rest of what went along with it before. And you do look good. It would have been a crime to waste that suit."

"Woo-hoo. Woo-hoo. Woo-hoo," Carter was still chanting when he came down the steps, holding on to the railing and carrying his coat under one arm.

"Okay, that's enough, big man," Lang said.

Still, Carter had to get in one more woo-hoo before he stopped.

"What are you guys up to tonight?" Lang asked, putting Carter's coat on and seizing the chance to change the subject.

"Mac and cheese, a movie on DVD, our special warm milk and bed." Livi recited what had apparently been a routine for the two of them when Livi had done her share of babysitting.

"Mac an' cheese!" Carter echoed this time, showing his enthusiasm. "I like it!"

Livi laughed. "I know you do."

"Wus go," the two-and-a-half-year-old said as soon as Lang had zipped up his coat and tied his hood.

"Hey," Lang said to Carter, feeling a little embarrassed to do what he was about to do in front of his sister. "Give me a kiss good-night."

It was something the toddler had instigated a few nights ago after watching one of his cartoons. The monkey in it had kissed everyone good-night before going to bed, and ever since then Carter had been demanding a good-night kiss after his bedtime story, before Lang turned off the light.

Lang had complied, thinking he was just doing it to appease Carter. But for some reason he couldn't explain, it was suddenly important to him, too. Important enough to do in front of his sister.

His sister, who was grinning from the sidelines as she watched Carter grant Lang's request with an exaggerated pucker.

But Livi didn't say anything about it. Which Lang was grateful for.

"You be good for Aunt Liv," Lang told the boy.

"Me an' Zsorzse," Carter amended.

"Yeah, you and George both be good and do what Aunt Liv tells you to."

"Eat-tin' mac an' cheese!" Carter confirmed.

Livi picked up Carter's backpack and took the toddler's hand. "We'll see you tomorrow at GiGi's. Don't forget tonight is business even though that suit is way, way too nice for work."

"All business," Lang repeated as he held the door open for his sister and Carter.

And yet as he glanced in the direction Heddy would be coming any minute, it wasn't business he was thinking about.

It was Heddy. Again.

Heddy, whom he was far more eager to see than he wanted to be.

And no amount of repeating to himself all the reasons why he needed to stamp out his attraction to her made the slightest bit of difference. He still couldn't wait to be with her again.

Maybe it would all just wear itself out, he thought. Maybe once he had her business up and running and they stopped having any contact, everything that was churning around inside him would just fizzle and die.

Which was what he wanted.

It was what needed to happen for everyone's sake.

And in the meantime he swore to himself that he was going to regain some control.

He just didn't know how he was going to do that when

there wasn't even a minute since she'd left the night before that he *hadn't* wanted his hands all over her again.

"I've been hearing about this place my whole life—it's nice to get to see it," Heddy said as she and Lang stepped out onto the terrace connected to the Denver Country Club's banquet room.

Behind them a five-piece band played music that they'd been dancing to since the auction had ended. The night had proved a triumph for Heddy's cheesecakes, which had garnered far more through bidding than she'd ever charged in her store.

Heddy and Lang had danced several times since then. Each time Lang had held her closer than the time before. Each time Heddy had been less and less conscious of the crowd. Each time she'd been more aware of having Lang's arms around her, of the feel of his big body against hers. And each time she'd looked up into those blue eyes and gotten a little more lost in them.

So when he'd asked if she wanted to get some air and see the country club's renowned golf course, Heddy had jumped at the idea.

"My mom is a golfer and playing here—being here—is something she's always talked about," she told him.

"My dad brought her," Lang said.

"That's the story," Heddy countered, unsure if they should get into this or not as they stood at the carved railing, looking out over the golf course her mother measured all other golf courses against.

Maybe Lang was unsure about broaching the subject, too, because for a moment neither of them said anything.

But then Lang broke the silence. "You told me that

your grandfather is okay with you doing business with us, but you didn't say how your mother feels about it."

Heddy shrugged a shoulder covered by the sparkly black shrug she was wearing over her sleeveless black dress. "Mom is a hundred percent against it," she said honestly.

They were standing side by side at the railing, both of them gazing out at the golf course, but from the corner of her eye Heddy saw Lang nod.

"Not a surprise," he said. And that was all either of them said for another few minutes before he ventured further. "So if she went on to a couple of jobs she hated after the bakery closed and then found something else for herself, what was the *something else?*"

"Mom went into nursing."

"Ah, and influenced you to do the same," he noted. "Did your parents meet through her job?"

"They did. My dad was an administrator at the hospital where my mom worked. It was about two years after the bakery closed."

"Did your mom like nursing and stay with it?"

"She liked it but when my brother and I were born she quit to stay home with us. Then, when I started school, she became the school nurse part-time so she was only away from home while my brother and I weren't there."

"And your parents have been happy together?"

Was he looking for absolution for his father?

Heddy knew that Kitty wouldn't give it if it was up to her, so she didn't feel free to. "My dad says she was pretty tough to get through to at first, but yes, they've been happy together since he finally did."

Another moment of silence passed before Lang said,

"She was tough to get through to because of the way things ended with my dad."

"She was really in love with your dad," Heddy said outright, deciding she wasn't going to skirt the issue anymore. "He left my mother for yours, didn't he?"

"Yeah," he admitted. "And there was some overlap that your mom found out about...."

"He and my mom were talking marriage," Heddy said. "My mom thought it was a done deal. That the ring and a formal proposal were on their way. She thought he might propose here, on this golf course, or at a fancy party. But just when everything was supposed to come together, the newspaper ran a picture of your father kissing someone else—that was how my mom found out he was cheating on her. With someone that the society page apparently considered a much more suitable match for him than 'the *little baker* he'd been seen with recently....'"

Heddy felt Lang flinch beside her. "I didn't know *that,*" he said. "That's how she found out? She saw a picture in the newspaper of him with my mother?"

"*Kissing* your mother. And with a caption that put *my* mother down," Heddy repeated because the insinuation that she hadn't been good enough for Mitchum Camden had caused Kitty additional pain and humiliation. "It hit her hard. It was one of those couldn't-believe-her-own-eyes things. But then she confronted your father and... well, the rest is history."

"We only found out recently about it."

"How could you only find out recently?"

"GiGi may have seen the picture in the newspaper at the time—I don't know about that—but it was only in the past year or so that we came across proof about what really went on with your mom and my dad. About how lousy my dad had handled things."

"Proof? Like letters?" Heddy remembered her mother saying that she'd written several scathing letters to Mitchum Camden condemning him for ruining her life and business.

"Actually it was something in my great-grandfather H.J.'s papers."

So not the letters. That was probably good. Heddy couldn't imagine that her mother would want letters like that read now, by people other than who they'd been intended for years and years ago.

"Not even GiGi knew at the time what my dad had done," Lang said then. "Or, believe me, she would have had something to say about it. GiGi has very high standards. She thought that things ended amicably between your mom and my dad *before* he met my mother." He paused another moment before he added with some reluctance, "And as far as GiGi or any of the rest of us knew until we read what H.J. wrote, the reason the Camdens stopped doing business with your family's bakery was just an inability-to-keep-up-with-demand issue. We thought that there was nothing personal in it."

"Except there was."

Lang didn't deny it.

So Heddy decided to push a little for her mother's sake. "My mom has always said that it was bad enough that Mitchum Camden cheated on her and *publicly* dumped her for someone else, but then he had to ruin Hanrahans Bakery on top of it because he couldn't face her, because he wanted to pretend she didn't exist anymore once he'd moved on."

"It isn't something that we'd let happen now," Lang replied, essentially admitting that her mother was right by again not offering a denial. "But we do a lot of things differently than the old guard did. If it helps, apparently my great-grandfather was pretty unhappy about losing Hanrahans bread. He really liked it."

Heddy laughed wryly. "My mother would not take comfort in that."

After her night at the Denver Country Club and her visit to Georgianna Camden's mansion, Heddy could see clearly the life her mother had been so sure she would be living, the future that Kitty had been convinced she'd have with the man she'd loved. It was a far cry from the suburbs and the public golf courses and the middle-class life that she'd ended up with. On top of that, Kitty had felt responsible for the failure of the Hanrahans Bakery.

"I'm sorry," Lang said, sounding genuinely contrite. "He was my dad and I loved him, but I have strong feelings about cheaters—it's kind of altered some of my thinking about him. But I also can't say that I'm sorry he ended up with my mom. I loved my mom, too. There's just nothing that makes what he did to your mom, and to your family's business, okay."

Lang turned to lean one hip on the railing, looking directly at Heddy's profile when he said, "I'm having some trouble being proud of him, that's for sure."

Lang turned the rest of the way around, leaning back on the railing and staring into the banquet room. And there was silence again, longer this time.

"On the other hand," he finally said in a lighter tone as

he nudged her shoulder with his. "Maybe it sounds selfish but if it all *hadn't* happened, you might not be here."

Heddy laughed. "My mom would probably agree that I was a good that came out of it. But my being *here?* I didn't even tell her about tonight because I knew she wouldn't like it."

Lang bent over and kissed her shoulder. "You, out here in the moonlight? There's nothing bad about that."

His soft words and kiss set off goose bumps, and Heddy leaned in his direction even when she knew she should be leaning away from him.

But before anything else could be done or said, someone took the auctioneer's podium inside to thank everyone for coming, signaling the end of the event.

Lang pushed off the railing to stand tall and straight in that suit that made him look better than any man had a right to look. "Guess we better go in and say some good-nights," he suggested.

Heddy agreed and stepped away from the view of the golf course. But as she did, she reminded herself that this was it. The evening ended here. That she had every intention of saying her goodbyes, then riding back to Lang's house and saying good-night to him the minute she got out of his car.

Before the feelings that had been churning inside her since last night had any chance of having their way.

Because tonight she was going to be smart.

Even if the dancing, the kiss on her shoulder, just being with him, were already weakening her resolve.

"Not a single taster left. Every cheesecake sold for top price. Believe me when I tell you that Maude Clark will be on the phone to GiGi by tomorrow morning trying to get her to convince you to cater the dessert for that party of hers. I think you were a hit."

Lang's voice broke into Heddy's thoughts as they drove away from the country club. He'd kept his hand at the small of her back as they'd exited the club, put his arm across her shoulders as they'd waited for the valet to bring his SUV, then helped her into the passenger seat. She wished she didn't like all the contact as much as she did but it was really all she could think about.

And now that she was alone with him in his car, the scent of his clean, citrusy cologne was going to her head, too....

*Cheesecakes. Think cheesecakes.*

"I'm glad it went so well," she said.

"Your future looks bright!"

A small, marveling laugh was her answer.

"What?" Lang asked.

"My *future,*" she mused. "It just hit me that for the past five years I haven't thought about a *future.* I guess I've just sort of *existed.* Even the shop was just a way of paying the bills, of getting by. Maybe that's why it failed. I didn't look at any kind of long-range projections because I haven't really seen beyond the here and now. I've buried myself in baking and sold what I baked to pay whatever bills came in when they came in, and that's been it for me."

"Living totally in the present. I know what you're talking about," he said, surprising her because he didn't seem to live that way, at least in terms of business.

"I've spent the past three and a half years not looking at the future, either," he said. "Just...well, I've called it 'living for the moment' because that sounds good, but the truth is, I've just done whatever I needed to do to get through each day."

"But now there's Carter."

"And not only do I have to think ahead to arrange nap times and meal times and bedtimes and bath times, but yeah, there's the bigger picture, too.... It's kind of opened things up for me, now that I think about it."

"And you've opened things up for me," Heddy said, realizing that she wasn't only referring to her business. The simple fact that she wanted him so much right now meant something was opening up for her that had been closed tight since she'd lost Daniel. Something she'd actually thought had died with Daniel.

But it was difficult to shut those feelings down now that they were back.

Maybe she could if she satisfied them....

What if she had just one time, with this one man? she asked herself. After all, he was the only one who had broken through her defenses. And he wouldn't be around forever.

Then she could go back to just being Daniel's widow.

*No, that was all dumb,* the voice of reason told her. They had arrived at his house and he was parking in his driveway. Her car was right there beside his, just waiting for her to get into it and go home, and that was what she was going to do!

It was the right thing to do....

Lang turned off the engine and got out, coming around to her side as she fumbled for the seat belt button and released it.

But when he held out a hand to her to help her out,

she took it before she'd thought better of it. Despite the fact that she didn't need help getting out of the SUV.

"It's not too late—barely eleven. It's Saturday night and Carter is with his aunt. How about coming in for a glass of wine?"

"I shouldn't," she said, to punish herself for having taken his hand—even though it felt so nice to have him holding hers still. "I know eleven isn't late but it isn't early, either, and I have to drive home."

It wasn't a firm refusal but he accepted it nonetheless, taking her around to the driver's side of her car.

She needed her two hands free to get her car keys out of her clutch. But she couldn't make herself take her hand out of his.

"Thanks for everything tonight," she said, gazing up into that exquisitely masculine face.

"Hey, I was the family delegate to this event, and you made it a whole lot more bearable than it would have been. Plus I think we stirred up some business for us both."

Business wasn't the only thing stirred up, Heddy thought as it occurred to her that Lang was the most handsome man she'd ever been that close to.

*Sorry, Daniel.*

But it was true. As much as she'd loved her late husband's boy-next-door good looks, they were nothing compared to the chiseled, ruggedly refined beauty of this guy.

Lang was staring down into her eyes so intently that Heddy couldn't recall what they'd been talking about mere seconds earlier. She was lost in that face, in those eyes that were so blue she could even see the color in the dim porch light. And again she wondered how whatever he'd stirred up in her was ever going to calm down again if she didn't find some kind of closure.

"I like your hair down," he said out of nowhere, sweeping the mass of waves over her right shoulder with his free hand. "I started imagining what it would look like the first day I met you—that's why I had to take it down last night. And tonight, when I first saw you and it was down…" He laughed at himself. "You'd think it was the first time I'd seen hair."

"It's usually just easier to put up, especially when I'm working."

"But it's so much sexier down," he whispered.

*Sexy?* She never thought of herself that way. But at that moment, under the heat of those blue eyes, she did feel a little sexy.

Enough to cock her chin up at him and smile a smile that didn't feel familiar.

A smile that brought a deliciously devilish one from him in return.

He pulled her toward him and leaned forward to kiss her.

And there she was, just like that, doing what she'd sworn she wasn't going to do again tonight.

But it was so good. And she liked kissing him so much. And she just couldn't make herself do anything but kiss him back, playfully, gladly, sexily….

His other arm went around her to hold her against him as their kiss took a turn and his tongue came to tickle the tip of hers before he paused only long enough to say, "Come in" and went back to kissing her.

She knew what was going to happen if she agreed. It

was all there, in that kiss. And in what she wanted and in what she could tell he wanted, too.

If she went into his house, there would be no turning back.

But through the haze of what she wanted, of what her body was shouting for, she recalled why she hadn't let this take its course the night before. She'd worried about following in her mother's footsteps and falling for a man she had no future with.

But she wasn't *falling* for Lang, she told herself. She just wanted him. Tonight. Just this once. Knowing there was no future in it. Not banking on anything. Merely taking it for what it was. One night….

It wasn't something she'd ever done before—a one-night stand. But if she'd lived the past five years only taking one day at a time, why did she have to start worrying about the long term right now? Why couldn't she have one more night of thinking only about the here and now? It wasn't dangerous if she knew there wasn't anything more to it than that….

Just the thought of what was on the verge of happening sent a shiver through her that Lang must have felt and interpreted as a chill because he held her closer, kissed her harder and again whispered, "Come in."

Only this time Heddy heard herself say, "Okay."

He laughed a little. "Really?"

"Just this once… Without it having anything to do with—"

"Anything but you and me," he finished, grinning down at her as if she'd just given him the best Christmas gift ever.

Then he took her to his front door, unlocking it in record time and letting them both into the dark house.

Once they were inside, he swung her around and into his arms to kiss her again as he kicked the door closed behind them.

And Heddy had one split second of doubt.

This wasn't Daniel....

But it *was* Lang.

Something about them being together just worked.

Effortlessly. Naturally. The way things between two people *should* work.

And somehow that overcame her moment of doubt.

Heddy raised her hand to the nape of Lang's neck and really did give herself to him as her mind emptied of everything else.

They went on kissing for a while before she realized she was still holding her clutch and let it drop to the floor.

As if that served as some kind of signal, Lang slid his hands under her open coat and the glittery shrug at once, finessing them off her shoulders, letting them drop to the floor, too.

Heddy kicked off her high heels, dropping down a few inches in height, forcing Lang to adjust his stance to maintain the kiss that was wide-open and hungry now.

He looked so fantastic in the suit he had on that Heddy almost hated to get him out of it. Almost. But the thought of what treasures might await her beneath it was good incentive, so she followed his lead, removing his overcoat and suit coat at the same time, slinging them over the stair railing that was just to his left.

His hands were in her hair, cradling her head as he

kissed her even more feverishly. She answered with a fever of her own every bit as intense. Their tongues played wantonly, and somehow the kiss went on that way even when Lang scooped her into his arms and carried her up the stairs.

Carter had shown her this part of the house when he'd given her the tour on Friday night. So Heddy knew when they reached the master suite even though the only light coming from outside was through the curtains at the three windows.

The room was huge, with a king-size bed bundled in a thick, downy quilt. Lang took her to the foot of the bed and set her on her feet again.

He yanked on his tie to pull it free, still craning forward to kiss her all the while. She also sensed that he was discarding his shoes and socks, though she was far more focused on letting her hands run the length and breadth of his broad back and wide shoulders while she answered his kiss and felt the cravings in her own body growing by leaps and bounds.

Her dress felt tight and confining, especially around breasts ready to explode out of the half-cup bra. She was only too happy when Lang—once he'd removed his tie and unbuttoned his collar—reached around to the back of her dress to unzip it.

Unzipping him was on her mind, too, but she was afraid that might be a little premature. So instead she tugged his shirttails from his waistband and then went to work on the rest of his shirt buttons—kissing, kissing, kissing him the whole time, their mouths magnetically attached and tongues hungry for each other.

He brought a hand to one of her breasts and she shuddered, recalling that first touch from the previous night, reliving and yearning to feel it again.

Oh, he had great hands! Big and strong and so, so adept.

She got rid of his shirt without ceremony, letting it fall to the floor because she couldn't wait any longer to press her hands to his naked skin.

Sleek, satiny skin over steely muscles that rippled under her flattened palms.

Her dress drifted down around her feet and she was left in bra and panties as he pulled her closer to him with one arm. Then his other hand found the breast that had been neglected so far.

To Heddy the bra might as well have been armor between them.

She laid her hands on his hard and honed pectorals. His own nipples were taut kernels, and she gave them some of the unbridled attention she was yearning for him to show her.

Then he unhooked her bra, slipped the straps down her arms and she got what she wanted as he filled one massive hand with her naked breast.

It felt so fantastic that she went slightly limp, losing track of the dance their tongues were doing and getting lost for a bit in the feel of that hand kneading, squeezing, massaging her bare breast.

And when he found her nipple with his fingertips, his gentle pinches and tugs and twirls turned that already tight little nib to a pebble of sublime sensation.

*Now* the zipper…

Her hands drifted down to his slacks. He was burgeoning behind that zipper, which she slowly lowered after figuring out how to release the hidden button at his waistband. A moan rose from deep inside Lang's throat as she finally set him free.

He helped her rid him of the slacks and whatever he had on under them, then swept her up into his arms to set her on that downy quilt that felt as if she were lying on a cloud.

He went to the nightstand drawer before joining her on the bed. While Heddy was grateful for the lack of light for herself, she was glad when he walked through a beam of moonlight that gave her a more illuminated view of him.

Incredible. That's what he was naked. Tall and lean, angular and cut and carved and more magnificent than she'd imagined him to be. She feasted on the sight even as she itched to touch him again.

Lying down beside her, he kissed her once more with a surprising chasteness for a moment before his lips and tongue trailed down the column of her neck, along her collarbone, then went lower, until he reached her breasts.

That first kiss, that first time that he took her into his mouth, brought Heddy's spine into an arch she couldn't suppress. Regardless of how adept he was with his hands, his mouth was even better.

Sweet suction and tender tugs of his teeth. Talented flicks of the tip of his tongue to the tip of her nipple. Warm, wet, feathery strokes. It all nearly set Heddy on fire, searing away any remnant of inhibition. And with that gone, she did what she was dying to do—she sent her own hand to press a path down his rock-solid abs to his long, thick, hard shaft.

A rumble of appreciation sounded from his throat

and he took her breast even farther into his mouth. One of his arms was curved above her head, his fingers in her hair. And as he went on driving her mad with that mouth, spending equal time on each breast, his other hand went on a slow, slow course down her stomach, down the outside of her thigh.

He paused at her knee, teasing her a little, somehow managing to send quick shots of lightning through her with just that touch. Then he went from her knee to her inner thigh where he traveled up again.

Heddy's breath caught in her throat in a tiny, high-pitched chirp when that hand traced the curve of her body, found entrance and slipped one finger, then two inside her.

Her grip on him tightened in response, as she slid her hand forward to the tip of his erection, then back to the base to drive him a little crazy, too.

Unfortunately it also drove him to abandon her breast, to abandon her completely while he made quick work of applying the condom. When he was done, he came back over to her and rediscovered her mouth with a kiss that was purely and completely erotic, that took her another step nearer to wanting him in every way she could possibly have him.

But he was suddenly gone once more. Down. His fabulous mouth finding that spot between her legs where his hand had been, his tongue flicking there, making Heddy writhe and moan in ways she never had in her life.

Then he came up again to kiss her on the lips, as he braced his weight, his hands flat on the mattress on either side of her head, arms straight.

Somehow he lured her tongue out with his, the tips

touching and teasing each other even as he found his way between thighs that opened and welcomed him all on their own.

He entered her, smoothly, slickly, and so, so divinely that she raised her hips to his to have all of him.

He began to move more deeply into her, pressing in so firmly that he reached a place she'd never felt before, then pulling out in slow motion. Then in so, so deeply again, angling his hips and hitting yet another spot that forced that chirp from her throat once more and made her hips push back at him.

He sped up, moving with the same method only more rapidly. Diving into her, pulling out. Diving in with that extra oomph just before he was out again. That extra oomph that she learned to meet.

With impeccable rhythm and timing, perfectly matched, they rode wave after wave. Each one taking Heddy nearer and nearer to what they were striving for. That peak that—when she reached it—was like an explosion inside her that rained shards of the most glorious, glittering pleasure, stealing her breath, stopping time, suspending her in a place she never wanted to leave.

Somewhere in the middle of that Lang reached his own pinnacle, intensifying hers even more and sending shudders of stronger pleasure through her, through him, melding them into one. Clinging to him, Heddy could only hang on as it all washed through her, over her, taking her will and setting her free.

And then it all began to ebb, and Heddy felt herself tumbling slowly down the other side of that peak. Drained and weak and supremely satisfied, she wilted under the weight of Lang.

Her arms were still around him and she pressed her palms over every inch of his hot, sweat-dampened back before she lost even that strength and her arms had to fall back to the mattress in complete surrender.

He kissed the side of her neck and dropped his forehead to the bed just above her shoulder, moaning softly.

Then, in a passion-raspy voice he said, "Where are your keys?"

"My keys?"

"Your car keys."

"In my purse. Downstairs."

He pushed himself up and away from her and walked toward the door.

Despite her confusion, Heddy reveled in the luscious sight of his naked backside, of a bare derriere so fine it was almost enough to get another rise out of her.

But then he was gone, and she felt as if she had become part of the quilt and didn't have the energy to move.

Instead she just lay there, listening to the sounds of him padding down the stairs then back up again.

From beneath hooded lids she stole another glimpse of the naked man whom Greek statues could have been modeled after.

He went to the head of the bed and flung the quilt and the covers aside. The next thing Heddy knew he was picking her up again then depositing her on the cool, crisp sheets that he crawled into with her.

He eased a long, muscular arm underneath her and rolled her as close to his side as he could get her. Close enough for her leg to fall over his before he yanked the blanket and quilt over them both.

"Your keys are hidden," he announced then.

Heddy laughed. "You're holding me hostage?"

"For tonight. Just for tonight. But yeah… There's no way I could let you get away from me tonight. Tomorrow I suppose I'll have to let you go. But tonight is mine. You're mine."

Heddy just laughed. She was too tired, too spent to argue even though she thought that she probably should. Plus there was another part of her that was already inching toward wanting him again and she couldn't put up any kind of fight that might prevent that.

So she just nestled her head into the hollow below one of his massive shoulders and closed her eyes.

"Okay, but anything after tomorrow and it hits the newspapers," she jokingly threatened. "The headline will be 'I Was Held Hostage by a Camden.'"

"'And Used as His Love Slave,'" Lang contributed, resting a warm hand on the outer curve of her bare breast.

"Or 'And I Made Him My Love Slave,'" she amended.

He laughed a throaty laugh. "Whenever you're ready," he said, bringing his other arm around to hold her even as she felt him relaxing into sleep.

## *Chapter Nine*

"No! Can't go down there! Immuh 'fraid. There's dragons an' hippos an' sheep down there!"

Lang closed his eyes, dropped his head forward and shook it in disbelief and frustration. It was Tuesday evening. He hadn't slept worth a damn Sunday or Monday night. He'd forgotten to do laundry and had to do it in a hurry when he and Carter had come home for the day. It had taken so long that Carter was late getting to bed while they'd waited for his pajamas to dry. And now the toddler's newest obsession was sucking up more time.

At GiGi's Sunday dinner Lang's brother Dane had brought Carter a DVD as a gift. An animated movie about a dragon. Lang had set it up for Carter to watch when he'd grown weary of the lengthy adult dinner the way he always did on Sundays.

No one had understood why Carter had been afraid of the kid-friendly dragon in the movie. He'd watched the entire thing hiding behind the sofa, merely peeking out to see what was on the screen, but pitching a screaming fit if anyone tried to turn it off.

Lang had no idea how hippos and sheep had been added to the fear list but ever since Sunday Carter had been insisting that he was afraid of all three, and that all three were hiding somewhere to get him. Mainly in places he didn't want to go anyway, but still, he was insistent.

"I can't leave you up here on your own," Lang told him. "You get into too much mischief. So come on, I'll carry you and I won't let any dragons or hippos or sheep… *Sheep?* Really? *Sheep?*"

"Sheep 'r *bad!*"

"Okay, I won't let any dragons or hippos or even sheep get you. I promise. But we need your pajamas so you can go to bed!"

Carter frowned at him but Lang had had a long day, so without further preamble he picked Carter up and headed for the basement laundry room.

"They're gunna git me!" Carter lamented, hooking an arm around the back of Lang's neck like a vise and hiding his face in Lang's shoulder.

"I won't let 'em get you. I would never let that happen."

"Can you fight 'em good as Ninzsa Tortle?" Carter whispered.

"I can," Lang said with confidence as, still holding the clinging toddler on one hip, he opened the dryer door, rummaged for what he needed and went upstairs again.

Once he had the little boy dressed and tucked into bed, Carter once more played the dragons, hippos and sheep card to get Lang to stay with him until he fell asleep. This, too, had been happening since Sunday night and Lang had now learned that it was easier and quicker to give in than to fight it.

"Okay, but you know the deal—no talking and you have to close your eyes."

Carter had learned the terms and did as he was told.

"Sit by my plillow," the closed-eyed Carter commanded.

Lang also did as he was told and sat with his back against the headboard. He rubbed Carter's brow to soothe him to sleep, sympathetic to the toddler's fears because he was wrestling with some fears of his own.

Of things that were much scarier than dragons and hippos…and sheep.

Since Saturday when Heddy had spent the night, he was scared out of his mind over what he was feeling for her. Over what he wanted. Over what he just couldn't stop wanting.

In fact, he'd spent the past three days in silent panic.

Regardless of how guarded—or according to his family, how closed off—he might have been before he'd met Heddy, she had somehow slipped in anyway. It was as if his feelings for her had developed and grown but camouflaged themselves enough to fool him into thinking that they were smaller than they were and that he could manage them. Control them. Walk away from them when the time came and have them dissolve.

Then they'd spent Saturday night together.

And the camouflage had dropped away and he'd been shocked to discover the extent of the feelings hiding behind it. There they'd been, bigger than he was.

He hadn't so much as called her since she'd left Sunday morning but he also hadn't thought about anything *but* her since then, either. And how much he wanted to hear her voice. To see her. To be with her. Every minute of every day and night.

Right at that moment he would have given his right arm to be able to walk out of Carter's room, down the stairs and find her waiting for him to spend the rest of tonight with…

*But what if she doesn't feel the same way?*

He couldn't shake *that* question any more than he could shake the rest of it. It had been jabbing at him alongside every single urge to call her, to see her, to be with her.

After all, he'd wanted Audrey as much as he wanted Heddy, and Audrey hadn't felt the same way about him. Hell, he wanted Heddy even more than he'd wanted Audrey. Which only meant that it could be even worse for him if Heddy didn't want him.

Worse.

And Audrey's rejection had been bad enough.

He really, truly, didn't think he could go through what he'd gone through again.

So for the past three days he'd been doing his damnedest to talk himself out of these feelings he had for Heddy. To make them go away.

Only nothing had worked. Not reminding himself that there was a bad history between their families. Not reminding himself that he had enough to deal with in terms of the newness of parenthood. Not reminding himself that he and Heddy had come together merely for business and that that was how it should have stayed.

Not even trying to find some kind of fatal flaw in her that could help stamp out the feelings.

Nothing.

If anything, every day that went by without seeing her, every hour, every minute, only made him want to be with her all the more.

He wanted her so damn bad it hurt.

And *that* reminded him of the way he'd felt after Audrey.

Full circle. Around and around he'd been going for three days.

He sighed in disgust with himself and glanced down at Carter.

Who was peeking up at him through the slit of just one eye.

"Close it," he ordered the toddler.

Carter wiggled around to reposition himself, tucked Baby under his chin and closed his eyes again. "Rub over here," he suggested, pointing to his cheek.

Lang smiled and buffed the soft skin of one chubby cheek with the back of his index finger.

And returned to those musings that he just couldn't escape.

He'd made it through the aftermath of Audrey and not only figured out how to go on, but also managed to find a way to want to. But not without a plan. A plan that demanded extreme caution. That demanded that he not go out on a limb for love again. And he'd been fine with that. It had worked for him for the past three and a half years.

Until Heddy.

And now he was a mess again.

How had this happened?

*This is the year for* that *question, isn't it?* he thought. First over Carter, now over Heddy.

But Carter had been an accident. A twist of fate.

He didn't know what Heddy was.

Except that she was great.

She was the complete package. Beautiful. Sweet. Kind. Funny. Easy to talk to, to be with.... And sexy as all hell without even knowing it.

Perfect.

She was perfect. At least for him. And Saturday night had cinched the deal because he'd never had a night as good as that one....

Another glance at Carter and Lang could tell the toddler was finally asleep. He carefully got off the bed and left the room, leaving the door only partially closed the way Carter liked it.

No, Heddy was not waiting for him when he got down the stairs. His living room was empty. And that was how it felt—everything without her felt empty. *He* felt empty without her.

"Damn!" He cursed himself as he swung through the desolate living room and went to the basement to get the rest of the laundry.

Where there were still no dragons or hippos or sheep.

But Lang's own fears were very real. And torturing him.

After Audrey he'd been in such a funk that he hadn't been able to see straight. He hadn't been able to work. He hadn't been able to get his brain to function enough to do anything but mope. He'd been lost. He'd had to figure out how to do just about everything in life on his own.

He'd gotten together with Audrey when they were both just kids. Fourteen. And not only had he loved her, he'd done everything from then on with her in mind. Or let her just do things for him.

She'd picked out his clothes. She'd told him how she thought his hair looked best. She'd kept track of all the birthdays in his family and usually recommended the gifts he should buy. She'd arranged their social life. She'd accepted or declined invitations. She'd basically done everything.

When she was gone, he'd had to step up his game on all of those fronts, too. So he'd been miserable *and* inept at pretty much everything except for his job.

"At least I'm not in *that* deep," he muttered to himself as he took the laundry upstairs to fold—yet another thing he'd had to figure out how to do after Audrey.

Which gave him another way to look at things.

Maybe he was grasping at straws, but what if now *was* the time to see if it could work out with Heddy *because* he wasn't in as deeply with her as he had been at the end with Audrey?

When it came to his feelings, he was already a goner—he wanted to deny that but he couldn't. So he gave in and just admitted it to himself—Heddy was in his blood and already being away from her made him miserable. He hated it, but he knew that if she wasn't in his life, it was going to be as difficult for him as losing Audrey had been. He cared for Heddy that much. He wanted her that much. If he couldn't have her it was going to kill him....

But if he took the leap now and got shot down, at least their lives weren't too entwined yet.

"That's some skewed logic," he said out loud.

Still it made a certain amount of sense to him. If she wouldn't have him, it would wipe him out emotionally. But at least at this early stage he could go on with the day-to-day. And hide what he was feeling.

The way he'd been hiding what he was feeling since Sunday morning.

But he was crazy about Heddy. He wanted her in his life. Permanently.

There was just no way around it.

And while he also had his hands full with sudden parenthood, the truth was that parenthood was better when Heddy was there, too. That the three of them made a better family than he and Carter alone did. That seeing Carter through Heddy's eyes helped him appreciate the little boy. It helped him have more patience and made him a better parent.

Everything was just better with Heddy along because she was the right fit. The perfect match. The complete package.

He was already all-in.

And the only chance he had to find out if she might be all-in, as well, was if he laid his cards on the table. If he told her what he wanted.

He just hoped to God that it was something she wanted, too.

Heddy was worried when she received a phone call from Lang at nine o'clock on Tuesday night asking if he could see her right away.

Of course she'd said he could come over—she'd been aching to see him since she'd left his house on Sunday morning.

But she'd also been a barrel of confusion since then and the insistence and anxiousness in his tone didn't help matters.

Knowing that she had about half an hour before he arrived, she threw on a better pair of jeans and a double layer of T-shirts. She reapplied the makeup she'd already washed off for the day and brushed her hair—leaving it the way she knew Lang liked it, long and loose around her shoulders.

Then she paced.

And agonized and felt guilty and excited all at once, wondering why Lang was suddenly on his way to her without explanation, after she hadn't heard from him since they'd slept together.

Was he coming to tell her that sleeping with her had been a mistake? And if that was the case, could it affect the grant or the arrangement to sell her cheesecakes to Camden Superstores?

She didn't think her business, her livelihood, could be ruined the way her mother and grandfather's bakery had been. She thought the paperwork protected her. But still it worried her.

So did the idea of him coming for more of what they'd shared on Saturday night.

She was just so confused.

For the past three days she'd been torn between aching to see him and feeling guilty and disloyal again. There had been a moment when she'd wondered if he might have been the worst thing to come into her life, the same as his father had been the worst thing to come into her mother's. Because why else would she feel so good and so horrible at the same time?

The sound of Lang's SUV pulling around to the rear of the house interrupted her fretting. She opened the back door before he'd even turned off his engine, then feasted on the sight of him when he got out of his car.

Tall and lean, broad-shouldered and commanding, dressed in jeans and a plain white crewneck T-shirt under a leather bomber jacket, he looked more incredible to her than anyone ever had before. Even as she told herself it probably would have been better if she'd never set eyes on him again.

He was carrying his smartphone out in front of him and talking into it as he headed for her. "Okay, here we go. We're on our way in."

Then he reached her and said, "Hi."

"Hi," she returned, her greeting having more of a question as she looked from him to his phone and back again.

When they went into the house, he turned to face her from the center of the living room as she closed the door. Then he resumed his phone conversation. "Are you guys with me?"

Two voices answered via the speaker on his phone. One male. One female. Both assuring him that they were indeed there.

Lang waved Heddy over and she went, curious.

"Say hi to Heddy," Lang instructed when she was close enough.

They did.

Then to Heddy, Lang said, "Say hi to Jani and Cade—he's at my house babysitting."

Heddy remembered that they were his cousins whom she'd met at his grandmother's house. "Hi, Cade. Hi, Jani…" she said with even more of a question in her voice as her confusion mounted.

Lang continued to address Heddy. "This is the formal transfer of the handling of the grant and all future business dealings between you and Camden Inc. From here on, Cade will be overseeing the grant, paying out the start-up money that hasn't already gone into the new facility and equipment, and making sure you have everything you need—all as we agreed. And Jani will work with you the rest of the way, with hiring and getting everything going both on your end and on ours. Okay?"

"Okay…" Heddy said tentatively.

"You guys on board?" he asked his cousins.

"Whatever you need," they said in unison.

"Then this officially ends my business connection with Heddy," Lang said. He handed Heddy two business cards: one Jani's, one Cade's, each with extra numbers written on the back. "I just gave her your cards, complete with cell and private landline numbers," he said into the phone.

Cade assured her that he would touch base with her tomorrow and Jani said she'd call in the morning and maybe they could have lunch. They both also told her to feel free to call them anytime for any reason, even at home.

"Okay… Thanks…" Heddy said, now even more confused.

Then Lang said, "That'll do it for tonight. Thanks, guys."

Goodbyes were made—with a "good luck" thrown in by Cade—before Lang ended the call and put the phone in his pocket.

"That was weird," Heddy said softly.

"I just wanted you to know up front that the business deal is still on. The grant, the help getting set up, the arrangement to sell through Camden Superstores—it's carved in stone. Nothing can or will change it, no matter what you say to me tonight."

"I just won't be doing business with *you*..." she said, feeling even more uneasy.

"No, you won't be," he said. "Because I want this—you and me—" He took her hand in his and pulled her to stand closer in front of him, keeping hold of it once she was. "To be strictly personal."

Heddy's concerns for her business future went away. But she was afraid to hear what he might have to say next because her own vastly mixed emotions put her at a loss for how she would respond.

"How are you?" he asked then, nothing business-like about him suddenly. "After Saturday night... Are you all right? You seemed all right Sunday morning."

When they'd made love for the fourth time before she'd left him.

"I know *I've* been a little nuts, so maybe you have, too?" he suggested.

"Why have you been nuts?" she asked to avoid answering his question.

He didn't beat around the bush. He seemed completely honest as he told her about being scared silly by what their spending the night together had unleashed in him. About the strength of his feelings for her. And as he confided in her, as he said wonderful things about her, she suddenly had the thought that this man standing in front of her was *her* Lang. The Lang she'd become familiar with, comfortable with. The Lang she'd gotten to know and to let know her. The Lang who had made it easy for her to be in awkward situations such as his family dinner and the auction at his country club. The Lang who had made love to her. The Lang she wanted to be with.

He was the Lang she'd been thinking about incessantly since she'd met him and even more incessantly since leaving him on Sunday morning.

The Lang whose arms she wanted to rush into right at that moment. The Lang whose lips she wanted to kiss. Whose hands she wanted on her. Whose naked body she wanted beside hers.

But as he went on to tell her what *he* wanted, to talk about a future with her, a future as a family—the worst of her buttons was pushed.

While he might seem like *her* Lang, she was desperately afraid that too much of her was still Daniel's wife. Tina's mother. And that she couldn't be all Lang was asking her to be.

"Oh. No," she said, interrupting him.

The *no* stopped him cold and his expression said it had hit him like a brick.

Heddy hated seeing that. Hated what she knew she'd just done to him, knowing that the other woman he'd cared deeply about had rejected him and now so was she.

"I'm sorry, Lang," she said with everything she

was feeling in her voice, with tears in her eyes. "I just can't—"

"You can. You've gone on since you lost your family, Heddy, and you have to keep going on. Do that with me!"

He was understanding. He'd been understanding all along. But he couldn't understand everything. He couldn't understand what Heddy wasn't sure she understood herself. The fear she had about moving *too* far away from Daniel and Tina. She couldn't do anything that made it seem as if they hadn't been the *most* important part of her life. As if they could be easily replaced. Or replaced at all. Ever.

Not even with Lang.

Or Carter.

"I can't go any further than I have," she said, her voice cracking. "I'm not sure I should have gone as far as I did…" She had to fight to keep from crying as guilt warred with that part of her that wanted this man and what he was asking of her. "It's just that you're so… You're great, you really are, and I sort of got carried away—"

"You just moved on, Heddy. The way you should have. The way you need to. We've both done enough of the just-existing-in-the-present thing because we've really still been attached to the past. Now it's time to have more. To have each other. And a future. Together."

She shook her head fiercely. "For me the past can't just be erased, Lang. That would be awful. I'm what's left of Daniel and Tina."

"I'm not asking you to forget them. They're a part of you and I know that. I'm okay with that. I'm just saying that that was an album of pictures from before. Now start a new album. Put that one someplace special to you, someplace that you can keep it with you, take it out and look at it again whenever you need to. But start a new album with me now."

And Daniel and Tina would just become what? Old pictures that barely meant a thing. That became irrelevant because they were from a different life, one that had been put up on a shelf eventually to be forgotten…

"I can't. I just can't!" she insisted, pulling her hand out of his and retreating until she had herself backed against a wall.

"Just think about it."

"No. I can't." Because to think about it might make her consider all she was saying no to. And how much she might want it… "I don't need to think about it. I just can't do it. I'm sorry. And if you want to pull the grant, if you don't want the cheesecakes—"

He shook his head, looking so good but so sad. "That's why we had that call before I started," he said in a low, deep voice that was gravelly with his own emotions. "The business is separate. We still want to sell your cheesecakes. That all stays the same, with Jani and Cade and whoever else will make it work the best way it can for you." He swallowed hard enough that she saw his Adam's apple bob. "It just won't go on with me."

*Not with him...*

Nothing would go on with him.

This was the end.

Heddy felt hot tears rolling down her cheeks but she couldn't stop them any more than she could turn her back on the ghosts of Daniel and Tina to be with Lang.

"I'm sorry," she whispered.

"So am I," he said softly in return, sounding every bit as bereft as she did.

Then he crossed to the door and left.

And that was when the real sobbing began for Heddy.

Sobbing just like she'd done for Daniel and Tina.

Only now it was for Lang.

And Carter.

And her.

## *Chapter Ten*

"Okay, I'm not going to let this happen," Clair said decisively. "I'm calling in the big gun."

"No! Don't—"

"Aunt Kitty? Would you come in here, please?"

Heddy had been caught by her cousin yet again. Dabbing at damp eyes. Putting her face in the freezer in the hope that the chill would keep them from swelling and turning red.

In the two weeks since she'd ended things with Lang and confided everything to her cousin, Clair had been with her through the numerous crying jags, the sudden bouts of out-of-nowhere tears that Heddy couldn't control. Having heard what Lang had said to Heddy two weeks ago, Clair's opinion had changed and she was strongly in favor of him. She'd talked herself blue in the face trying to convince Heddy to put everything behind her and go to him, to change her no into a yes.

But it hadn't worked.

And now, after Clair and Kitty had spent their Saturday helping Heddy take her shop apart, Clair found Heddy in silent tears once again and had apparently reached the end of her patience.

"Don't tell her!" Heddy whispered to her cousin just as Kitty came from the shop into the kitchen.

But Clair ignored Heddy's command and laid the whole thing out for Heddy's mother.

"I knew it! I knew you were going to fall for that man and that something was wrong," Kitty said when Clair was finished. "You've been owlish and quiet and sad, and I knew it wasn't over Daniel and Tina. Plus I wondered why I wasn't hearing anything about Mitchum's son anymore and why Jani and Cade Camden were coming up instead. They took over for him?"

They had. Just the way everyone had promised. Cade had overseen the closing on the commercial kitchen that was now in Heddy's name and fully paid for. He'd made sure the equipment she and Lang had picked out had been delivered and also paid for in full. He'd dealt with legal papers of incorporation that would help Heddy with taxes, as well as setting her up with business managers.

Jani had been working with her on everything else—implementing the next stages of Lang's start-up plan. She'd helped interview staff. She'd talked Heddy through the basics of running a large-scale operation. She'd introduced her to the purchasing people she would be dealing with on a regular basis with Camden Superstores. And she'd generally helped to put her in a position where she would be able to accomplish what was turning into a much bigger endeavor than Heddy had realized it would be.

"Yes, they took over for him," Heddy confirmed as she and Clair and Kitty sat around the kitchen table.

Heddy deflated considerably from the overly cheery front she thought she'd been showing her mother up to that point and merely fought to keep from crying again. But in spite of all it was taking to maintain her composure, she saw her mother mentally pondering what she'd just learned, weighing it and then seemingly coming to some sort of resolve that straightened her spine and made her sit up stiffly.

"So history did repeat itself," she said then. "There's something about those Camdens. I just knew he was going to get to you. But this one was serious?"

"Serious enough for *me* to have hurt *him,*" Heddy lamented.

"And obviously you love him," her mother stated matter-of-factly.

Heddy didn't say anything to that because she'd been trying not to think about it. Trying not to admit it to herself. As if that would make it untrue.

"And *I* love *you,*" Kitty said sternly, "and I want you to be happy. I want you to have a full life. Like you had with Daniel. But just because you had that with Daniel doesn't mean you can't have it again, with this man—if it has to be with this man."

"She thinks she'll be erasing Daniel and Tina completely if she doesn't keep herself as some kind of shrine to them," Clair said, voicing her perspective.

"Well, that's not true," Kitty said definitively. "The

awful truth is that Daniel and Tina aren't with us anymore, and sacrificing yourself to their memory? That isn't going to bring them back. That's just going to be wasting your own life. And I won't let you do that!"

Heddy laughed sadly. "Now you're pushing for me to be with a Camden?"

"I'm not thrilled that he's a Camden," Kitty said in no uncertain terms. "But I want you to be happy. You *deserve* to be happy again. And if a Camden is what it takes, then I'll live with it."

"There would have to be interaction between you and Lang, between you and the rest of the Camdens..." Heddy pointed out.

"Today's Camdens aren't responsible for what was done to your grandfather and me," Kitty said, as if she'd given this some thought even before now, and as if maybe Heddy's grandfather or her father might have had some input. "I'll keep that in mind. I'll also keep in mind that today's Camdens have done right by you. And if this Lang character behaves himself and treats you well and you can have a good life with him? Then that's what counts for me. We'll let the rest be ancient history."

Kitty Hanrahan stood and hugged Heddy where she sat in the kitchen chair. "Get me and your dad on that country club golf course again and I'll even think about forgiving them," she added.

Heddy laughed but felt her eyes well up once more when her mother continued.

"This doesn't mean you're forgetting Daniel and Tina. Hold them in your heart. We all do. But it's your life that's left. And you need to go on with it."

"Which is what I keep telling her!" Clair said.

"Easier said than done," Heddy muttered in a cracked voice.

"But it needs to be done just the same," Kitty decreed.

Kitty and Clair both had to get home then. Heddy said her goodbyes still sitting at the table. Thinking. Awash with emotions.

It helped to have her mother's approval. It was good to know that a rift in the family wouldn't be caused one way or another.

But it didn't take away all of Heddy's misgivings. She still had a sense that she belonged to Daniel and Tina. And to give herself over to someone else, to Lang, to Carter, was to somehow admit that Daniel and Tina were gone once and for all.

What her mother had just said, what Clair had also been telling her for the past two weeks, *did* take some of the weight off her shoulders, though. And pushed Heddy to come to new terms with the facts.

The hard, harsh truth was that Daniel and Tina weren't coming back.

And not giving herself over to Lang and Carter didn't change that. It just left Heddy alone. With her memories. With some pictures. But with nothing else.

Memories and pictures that wouldn't go away if she did make Lang and Carter her family.

And Heddy decided that maybe it was time she heard the message that everyone was trying to send. Embraced it.

And did actually move on.

With Lang.

Lang.

Just the thought of him, of the look on his face when she'd turned him down, the thought that she'd hurt him the way she had, the thought of not having him for the past two weeks or now or maybe ever, put her close to tears again.

She missed him so much!

And she hated that she'd hurt him.

And she wanted to see him so badly that it hurt her.

So what was she doing? she wondered. Was she punishing herself? Would suffering the way she had since the last time she'd been with Lang bring Daniel and Tina back?

Of course it wouldn't.

So what was the point?

To be some kind of long-suffering widow?

That phrase made her smile.

Daniel had always joked when the inevitable conversation had come up about one of them outliving the other. He'd always said she was his and no one else could have her, that she would just have to be a long-suffering widow.

But it *had* been a joke. And while he might not have wanted anyone else to have her when he was alive, she knew without a doubt that he also hadn't ever wanted her to be unhappy or miserable. The way she was now without him *and* without Lang.

And Lang was right here. Now. Wanting her.

Or at least he had two weeks ago.

And somehow she suddenly knew deep down inside that even Daniel wanted her to do something about that. Something better than what she'd already done.

"I won't forget you. Neither of you. Not ever," she said into the air, speaking to her late husband, her lost little girl.

And of course she *wouldn't* forget them. Or love them any less than she had when they were alive, than she had since losing them.

But she also loved someone else now, too. Two someone elses. Lang and Carter. Without taking anything away from what she'd had, what she'd felt for Daniel and Tina.

This was just that new album that Lang had talked about her starting. An album she knew she needed to start for her own sake.

An album she wanted to start.

And fill with new pictures while she still held that old album and those old images near and dear to her.

Unless it was too late…

She hadn't heard a single word from Lang since he'd left here that Tuesday night. Cade hadn't so much as mentioned him. Jani had said only that Lang had given her step-by-step instructions of where to go with the business. Nothing else.

He'd made good on his word when it came to business, but that didn't mean that he didn't hate her.…

Still, she decided that she couldn't let even that possibility keep her from going to him. From apologizing to him. From seeing him again and at least trying to make some amends of her own.

And if he shot her down?

She hoped he wouldn't.

But in spite of that possibility, she had to put herself

in the line of fire to find out if there was any chance at all that they might actually have that future he'd offered her before.

"Heddy..."

"Hi..."

That was the extent of the exchange at Lang's front door when he opened it after Heddy rang his doorbell that Saturday evening.

Then, before she could say anything, a stark-naked Carter charged around Lang's legs and ran out of the house as Lang stood there frozen in surprise, staring at Heddy.

"Oh, Carter!" she said when she found her voice, being the first to step into action to grab the toddler's hand before he could get off the front stoop.

His hair was damp and even though it was a nice April night, it wasn't warm enough for the child to be outside without clothes on and with a wet head.

Apparently that finally registered with Lang because he quickly ushered Heddy inside with the little boy, closing the door behind them.

Then he picked Carter up from Heddy's grasp and held him like a football against his side. Facing the floor, his tiny round rump in the air, the toddler was giddily laughing.

"Hi..." Lang belatedly answered Heddy's greeting, his tone full of questions.

"I'm sorry to just show up," Heddy said, still unsure what to say at all, having not been able to come up with something smooth and clever in the hours since her mother and cousin had left or on the entire drive to Cherry Creek. "If you have plans—"

"I plan to put this wild child to bed, but that's it," Lang said.

Heddy had worried that she might come here and find him with a date. Or out on a date. Or dressed in that gray suit he'd worn to the country club, looking amazing, and on his way out the door to pick up a date.

Even in a pair of old jeans and a nondescript, tan crew-necked sweater with the sleeves pushed up to his biceps, he still looked amazing to her. And she was terribly relieved that none of her date scenarios were true.

"I wondered if we could talk..."

"Okay," he said, sounding leery and not altogether eager to hear what she had to say. "I just have to get him into his pajamas and read him to sleep—"

"Hetty read'a me!" Carter demanded from Lang's side, just to be contrary.

"Or you could read him to sleep," Lang said.

"Sure," Heddy agreed, grasping at straws and hoping that maybe by the time Carter nodded off she would know what to say to Lang.

All adult focus went to Carter from that moment until the little boy was snoozing in his bed. Then Heddy and Lang tiptoed out of Carter's room and made their way downstairs to the living room without speaking. Heddy was still too worried that he might have changed his mind about her and clueless as to how to tell him what she'd come to tell him.

"Want to sit down?" he asked when they reached the living room.

"I don't think I can," Heddy answered, stopping just

inside the entrance to the room and suddenly sounding every bit as nervous as she felt in spite of the care she'd put into her own appearance. She'd showered, shampooed her hair and left it wavy and loose. Then she'd put on her best-fitting jeans and the two layers of body-hugging T-shirts—navy blue over white—that showed off the benefits of her best-fitting bra.

Lang went farther into the room to sit on the arm of the white leather sofa, facing her, watching her, waiting.

"This is really hard," Heddy muttered.

"Did you come to complain about Cade or Jani? Are they not doing something the way you want it done?"

"No! They're great," she assured him. "This isn't business. What's between you and me is only personal, remember?"

She was making reference to what he'd said when he'd showed up at her house with Jani and Cade on the speaker of his smartphone. But she just thought what she'd said sounded dumb.

"I thought you didn't want anything else personal between us," Lang pointed out.

"Yeah. I know that's what I said..." She swallowed, reminded herself that *she'd* rejected *him* and now the only way to put this back together—if there was any chance at all—was for her to be open and honest with him. And run the risk of being rejected herself.

So she sighed and said, "It might sound ridiculous or stupid or something, but even after I lost Daniel and Tina I still kept telling myself that I was—and would always be—Daniel's wife, Tina's mom..." She shrugged and wondered why she'd gotten so overly emotional again when tears threatened at just saying those words. "I guess it sort of helped me get through the past five years and let me go on feeling…I don't know, connected to them. Then you came along and…" Another shrug. "I guess a part of me went back to just being Heddy and that part of me…"

*Just say it!* she ordered herself.

"I did what I didn't think I could ever do again, with anyone else," she said very softly. "I fell in love with you."

"And then found a whole world of guilt." Lang supplied the words for her.

"Yeah. And the worst feeling that I was being disloyal."

"Disloyal?" He laughed a humorless laugh. "You've been loyal to people who haven't even been here for the past five years. I'd say you're one of the *most* loyal people I've ever known."

"It just isn't easy, you know?" she said, opening up to him the way she'd come to do over the course of getting to know him.

"Giving in to what I feel for you," she said then, "letting myself have a future with you, was putting an end to them, to what I had with them, which was more than I could let myself do. If that makes any sense at all…"

"It does, actually," he said quietly.

"But the past two weeks…" she continued. "I lost you, too. And Carter. And that caused me to do a whole lot of crying and moaning to Clair, who finally brought my mother into the picture this afternoon and…" Yet another shrug. "When my mother got on board with me moving on even if it meant moving on with a Camden, I knew I had to think about some things."

"Ah, the evil Camdens," he said, not seeming to take offense.

"She conceded that the Camdens of today aren't who did her wrong. I wouldn't say that she's forgiving anything—particularly your father or what he did or the way he handled it—but she is excusing the rest of you from blame and giving you all a pass," Heddy said, managing a small smile as she relayed that news. "And I think I have to give myself one, too. Or permission, maybe, to go on, to have what I want now."

"Which would be…?"

He knew. She could see it. But she could also see that he needed to hear it. Hopefully not just so he could throw it back at her.

"You," she said. "I want you. And a life with you. And with Carter. A home together. Even other kids…" Though that last part was especially difficult for her to say.

Lang seemed to understand how hard it was for her. He stood and came to her then, taking her upper arms in his hands, offering comfort and support.

"You can plaster the walls with pictures of them both, if you want. We can set places at the table for them at every meal. They can be as much a part of us as you need them to be, if there can just *be* an *us*."

God but she loved this man…

Her eyes welled up again and she shook her head while she blinked back the tears.

"Don't make me out to be *too* crazy," she said. "It's enough that you aren't asking me to act as if they never existed, that I don't have to be afraid of talking about them or mentioning them. That you recognize and honor that they were my life before you…" She looked up into those warm blue eyes of his. "But now I want to have a life *with* you. If that's still what you want."

He dropped his head forward and pressed his lips to her hairline, then breathed out a hot gust of air before he said, "I love you, Heddy. So yeah, it's still what I want. More than I could even begin to tell you."

Tears again. She really had become a soggy mess. But once more Heddy blinked them away and, through a clogged throat, said, "I love you, too."

She tipped her head back, away from his so she could look at him, and he kissed her. A long, deep kiss where passion blossomed and grew.

But before it went too far Lang ended the kiss, wrapped his arms tightly around her and pulled her up against him so closely that—with her head pressed to his chest—she could hear his heartbeat.

"You'll stay? Tonight and maybe from here on?" he asked her.

"I'll stay tonight. Beyond tonight—we'll have to talk about that."

"Good because I'm going to spend the whole night ravaging you."

Heddy smiled. "Okay."

"But for now I just want to hold you."

"Also okay. Really, really okay," she said, her arms wrapped around him, holding him as tightly as he was holding her.

"And you'll marry me?" he asked as if he were only confirming it.

In for a penny, in for a pound.

But still it was with a hint of guilt and a twinge of disloyalty that she said, "I will."

"We don't have to rush," he said softly, again understanding that getting all the way to the altar with someone other than Daniel would not be easy for her. "Whenever you're ready. But I want us to at least be engaged. To be together."

"Me, too," she said, knowing that the longer they were engaged without getting married, the more it would worry him, the more it would remind him of the woman who had strung him along only to dump him rather than become his wife. And she appreciated that he was setting aside feelings that had to be difficult for him just to help her.

But as she stood there in his arms, Heddy knew that she would only need a little time to get used to the idea of actually becoming Lang's wife. She just wanted it too much herself. She wanted him too much.

And she could only hope that if Daniel was looking down on her, he was as understanding as Lang was.

But she had the sense that he was. That he wouldn't have wished her to have an entire lifetime of living the way she'd lived for the past five years, of clinging to a past that was lost, of barely existing in the present. And she thought that Daniel would be glad that she'd found happiness again.

And she had.

"I do love you, Lang," she whispered again, the feelings she had for him welling up inside her now rather than tears.

"I know. I can feel it," he joked, holding her even tighter, almost melding their bodies together.

But what he didn't know was that she loved him more than she'd thought she could ever love anyone again.

This man who came complete with a little boy. A little boy she loved, too, for himself and for every glimpse—even those shadowed with pain—that he gave her of what Tina might have been like.

And while she knew that she would never totally escape the sadness of losing Daniel and Tina, while she would always love them and miss them, while no one could ever replace them, she also knew in that moment that becoming a family with Lang and Carter was the gift of a second chance.

A gift she'd turned away once.

But would never ever turn away again.

* * * * *

Every month we put together collections and longer reads written by your favourite authors.

Here are some of next month's highlights— and don't miss our fabulous discount online!

On sale 6th September

On sale 6th September

On sale 16th August

Find out more at
**www.millsandboon.co.uk/specialreleases**

*Visit us Online*

0913/ST/MB433

# *Join the Mills & Boon Book Club*

Want to read more **Cherish™** books?
We're offering you **2 more** absolutely **FREE!**

We'll also treat you to these fabulous extras:

- **Exclusive offers and much more!**
- **FREE home delivery**
- **FREE books and gifts with our special rewards scheme**

***Get your free books now!***

**visit www.millsandboon.co.uk/bookclub**
**or call Customer Relations on 020 8288 2888**

**FREE BOOK OFFER TERMS & CONDITIONS**
Accepting your free books places you under no obligation to buy anything and you may cancel at any time. If we do not hear from you we will send you 5 stories a month which you may purchase or return to us—the choice is yours. Offer valid in the UK only and is not available to current Mills & Boon subscribers to this series. We reserve the right to refuse an application and applicants must be aged 18 years or over. Only one application per household. Terms and prices are subject to change without notice. As a result of this application you may receive further offers from other carefully selected companies. If you do not wish to share in this opportunity please write to the Data Manager at PO BOX 676, Richmond, TW9 1WU.

JBS/ONLINE/S1